"Absolutely amazing. Unique plot and characters, great pacing, and as usual wonderfully sensual! This book had everything I absolutely loved, and stood for what I and anyone would want in a relationship. Enduring love, and it was so so sweet and good." -Sara, *Goodreads*

"A page turning romance. I loved the fact that the story goes back and forth in time to tell the story of this couple's romance. You feel the betrayal and live through their bitter separation, and rejoice in their reconciliation!" -Kathy, *Goodreads*

"A captivating ensemble that had me on an emotional rollercoaster glued to the end." -Nicola, *Goodreads*

"This is the kind of story that a reader must experience him/herself in order to fully enjoy it. Just know that the author did an incredible job showing how marriage is a two-way street and how both partners must equally give and take in order for it to work. The author did an excellent job with the characters and how their lives were changed and reshaped for the better after Pandora's secrets were out. Again, I don't want to explain anything in detail because I would just ruin this beautiful story." –*Romance Library*

"Thoroughly enjoyed being on the edge of my seat with the love/mystery mix." -Gidget, *Bookbub*

"Penny is an incredibly strong character. I especially liked when the integration of her past and present occurs and she decides to take control of events rather than groveling as to her lies. I like that this story is about Penny becoming her true self even as Marcus discovers the true woman he has loved and married." -Sheila, *Goodreads*

"I really liked this one. It wasn't about finding love, but about reclaiming it. The heroine's dark past caught up to her and looks to destroy her marriage. I liked that you could feel the angst and the uncertainty on each side. The wanting to reconnect but the fear of betrayal and the broken trust. I thought it was a wonderful book." -Kag, *Bookbub*

"This Christmas novel has all of the GC hallmarks: strong, broody heroes, stronger, badass heroines, remarkable friendships that leap off the page, drama, and some pretty wild regency era sexy times. And I LOVED that the couple was in their 30s/40s and had been married for 12 years. Such a different pair than we usually see in regency romance." -Eliza, *Goodreads*

"This is one book where complex, dark emotions coupled with deep exploration of trust, self-worth, and self-acceptance pays off tremendously. Kudos to Callaway for the witty dialogue, refreshing, yet believable storyline, and wonderful writing of those said complex, dark emotions." -Amazon Reviewer

"I loved this story of a happily married couple who have a crisis in their marriage because of secrets kept. It was sexy, emotional and thought provoking." -Karinannah, *Bookbub*

ALSO BY GRACE CALLAWAY

LADY CHARLOTTE'S SOCIETY OF ANGELS

Olivia and the Masked Duke

Pippa and the Prince of Secrets (Fall 2021)

GAME OF DUKES

The Duke Identity

Enter the Duke

Regarding the Duke

The Duke Redemption

The Return of the Duke

HEART OF ENQUIRY (The Kents)

The Widow Vanishes (Prequel Novella)

The Duke Who Knew Too Much

M is for Marquess

The Lady Who Came in from the Cold

The Viscount Always Knocks Twice

Never Say Never to an Earl

The Gentleman Who Loved Me

MAYHEM IN MAYFAIR

Her Husband's Harlot

Her Wanton Wager

Her Protector's Pleasure

Her Prodigal Passion

THE *Lady* WHO
CAME IN FROM THE COLD

HEART *of* ENQUIRY

GRACE CALLAWAY

USA Today Bestselling Author

Cover Design Credit: Erin Dameron-Hill/ EDH Graphics

Cover Image Credit: The Killion Group

FRANCE, 1813

At the sound of her bodice ripping, Pandora clenched her teeth and pushed away the soldier's groping hands. *Blooming hell. My mission's going to be foiled—by a bleeding foot wabbler?*

It was her own dashed fault. She should have been more careful. Her disguise as a trull—a camp prostitute—was a double-edged sword. On the one hand, it gave her access to the army encampment; on the other, it made her appear fair game to the lusty, drunken foot soldier presently accosting her. She'd chosen the dark path at the edge of the camp to avoid such pitfalls, but the bounder had stumbled out of nowhere.

"Let's warm ourselves with a tickle, eh dove?" he leered, his words puffing in the wintry night. "Share some real Yuletide cheer?"

In the cold moonlight, she saw his glazed eyes and unshaven face, and her stomach lurched at his stench of liquor and unwashed flesh. Memories of another time rose like a dark tide, but she pushed them back. At nineteen, she was no longer a helpless girl. She'd killed men far stronger and cleverer than the bastard in front of her.

In fact, she'd done so not a quarter hour ago.

Which left her with a problem: she couldn't afford to leave *another* dead body in the camp. One fatality might be attributed to natural causes (certainly the poison she'd used was designed to mimic death from a heart ailment). Two corpses, however, would definitely rouse suspicion.

A good spy leaves no incision, Octavian always said. *In and out.*

Octavian was her mentor, the man who'd plucked her from the gutters and given her a new life and purpose—and the tools with which to practice her new trade. He'd even given her a new identity: *Pompeia.* She was the only female agent that he'd recruited into his elite espionage ring, and it was an honor and privilege she did not take lightly.

No, she wouldn't let Octavian down... which meant no more killing for the night. She'd have to brazen her way out of the situation. Luckily, she had some skill at dealing with the opposite sex.

Planting her palms firmly against her attacker's chest, she used the Cockney of her childhood. "Another time, luv. Got a couple o' brats in me tent squallin' for their supper."

Nothing like the mention of children to throw ashes on a man's libido.

"Let 'em wait. I'll feast my fill, then they can 'ave theirs, eh?" Smirking, he cupped her bottom and squeezed.

Disgusting. She slapped his hand away, moved out of reach.

Feigning an apologetic look, she said, "'Fraid there's another problem, sir. I've a fire on board." She waggled her brows. "Wouldn't want your mast to get burned by the flames."

If the threat of venereal disease wasn't enough to stop him, nothing was.

"Only one thing to lower my mast tonight. Fire or not, I'm coming in," he slurred.

He launched himself at her, and she took an instinctive step backward, only to trip on a blasted rock. Her breath left in a whoosh as her back hit the frost-hardened ground. He wasted no time in clambering atop her, fumbling to push her skirts up.

"No," she gritted out. "Stop it. Get off me, you bastard."

He didn't take any notice.

Blast it. He left her with no choice. She'd have to choke him unconscious; mayhap when he came to, he'd forget what happened, think he'd passed out in the dark. It wasn't the clean exit she'd hoped for, but it was a damned sight better than getting raped in the dark. Digging the heels of her boots into the dirt, she readied to leverage her strength, to reverse their positions so that she could plant her arm against his windpipe and cut off his supply of air.

Just as she tensed to act, her attacker's weight suddenly disappeared. Blinking, she watched him hurtle backward into the darkness. The next second, she scrambled to her feet and saw that another figure had materialized: this one was tall, broad-shouldered—and strong, by the looks of how easily he subdued her assailant. After a brief grapple, he twisted his opponent's arm and used it to drive the other to his knees. The soldier cursed and moaned but couldn't escape.

"I could have you court-martialed for this," the stranger snapped.

His captive stopped struggling instantly. "Lieutenant-Colonel Harrington. *Sir.*" Though still slurred, the soldier's voice now held a note of fear. "I-I didn't know it was you. B-beg pardon—"

"Bradley, is it?"

Even in the dimness, Pandora saw the reluctance of Bradley's nod. "Y-yes, sir."

"It isn't my pardon you should be begging." Harrington released Bradley with a shove, his gaze locking on her. "Are you all right, miss?"

"I'm fine," she managed.

She'd seen too much, known too much to be surprised by

anyone. But Lieutenant-Colonel Harrington was unlike any man she'd ever met. She knew his name, of course; anyone who kept abreast of England's struggles with Napoleon did. Over the past few years, he'd become one of the nation's heroes because of the courage and valor he'd shown on the battlefield. Just twelve days ago, he'd been part of Lieutenant-General Hill's valiant efforts to stave off the French attack at St. Pierre. It was rumored that Wellington planned to bestow a commendation upon Harrington.

What surprised Pandora wasn't just Harrington's youth (he looked to be in his mid-twenties—young for an officer of his rank and achievements). No, it was also the fact that this much-lauded hero was addressing her as courteously as if she were some Mayfair debutante and not the painted strumpet she was currently disguised as. His fierce eyes—she couldn't tell their color in the dimness—stayed on her face and didn't wander to the expanse of flesh displayed by her torn bodice.

"See? N-nothing 'appened, sir." Stumbling to his feet, Bradley rubbed at his arm, his voice just short of a whine. "We were just 'aving a bit 'o fun—"

"It didn't sound like fun to me." Harrington's tone had a dangerous edge that raised the hairs on Pandora's skin—and, intriguingly, not in a bad way. "I heard the lady tell you no. She told you to stop."

Blanching, Bradley nonetheless said unwisely, "But she's just a trull—"

"And that gives you the right to assault her?" Harrington demanded.

"N-no, sir, I didn't mean... that is..."

"We are fighting a war to protect those who cannot protect themselves. As soldiers, this is our duty. What does it say about you that you'd take advantage of someone weaker and less powerful than you?"

Weaker and less powerful? Pandora stifled a snort. If she'd chosen to employ her trusty garotte, she could have strangled Bradley before he could let out so much as a squeak. Nevertheless, she couldn't help but be charmed by Harrington's moral code. His chivalry was rather quaint, like that of a knight of old. As much as she enjoyed watching him make that worm Bradley squirm, however, she couldn't allow matters to get even more out of control. She had to contain the situation. *In and out.*

"No 'arm done, sir." She addressed the Lieutenant-Colonel with a whore's pragmatic cheeriness. "Just a misunderstanding is all. Be obliged if you'd let the lad off—if word gets out 'round camp, it'll be bad for business, if you get my meaning."

Harrington's gaze roved over her, so intently that for an instant she fancied that he could see through the curly blond wig designed to distract from her features, the layers of paint she'd meticulously applied, the torn and tawdry dress. That he could somehow see *her*...

Her heart quickened; her breath jammed in her throat.

Turning to Bradley, Harrington said curtly, "Report to my tent at eight o'clock sharp. You're dismissed."

Like a cur with his tail between his legs, Bradley slunk off.

Harrington advanced toward her, unbuttoning his scarlet jacket. Immediately, Pandora took a step back, but he was too quick for her. He reached out... and a moment later, she was engulfed in warmth and a clean, masculine scent.

The cove gave me his jacket? She blinked up at him, bemused.

"I'll walk you back to your tent," he said.

"No. That is, no need, sir." She gathered her wits. "I'll find my own way back—"

He took her arm, his grip on her elbow gentle yet firm. "It's dark. You shouldn't be out alone at night. It's not safe with a battalion of soused soldiers roaming about."

Did he not see that she was dressed and painted like a whore? Where else would she be but plying her trade in precisely such circumstances? Before she could think of a reply, he was steering her through the darkness toward the cluster of small, glowing tents in the distance, home to the camp followers.

"May I ask your name, miss?" he said.

Blooming hell.

"It's Kitty, sir. Kitty, um,"—her gaze latched on a clump of dead bushes—"Brown."

"Marcus Harrington, at your service. I must apologize, Miss Brown, for my subordinate's behavior. Rest assured he will be punished for his offense."

She slanted a look at Harrington. His dark hair was cut in a short, no-nonsense style, and his features were too rough-hewn and stern to be handsome—but handsome was too paltry a word to describe a man with such an aura of command. No, a more apt adjective was... compelling. Disturbingly masculine. Magnetic to the senses.

This isn't a promenade through Hyde Park, you stupid chit. Focus. You've got to get out of here.

"Be obliged to you, sir, if you left it alone. Like I says before, a girl's got to make her livin'. If talk spreads,"—she looked up at him through heavily sooted eyelashes—"I'll be out o' work."

"Would that be so bad?"

She heard no judgment in his voice. Just a calm curiosity.

Shrugging, she said, "Do what we 'ave to do to survive, don't we, guv?"

In her case, that meant protecting her country by any means necessary. Something that he'd never find out. Octavian's warning rang in her head. *Military and espionage are like oil and water: the two don't mix. Those mushrooms in uniform are too stodgy to trust us, and we're too clever to trust them.*

"One can't argue against the importance of survival." Harrington's lips formed a tight line. His was a nice mouth, if a trifle stern. "Yet every profession has its downside."

She tilted her head at him. "Even yours?" He was a respected officer of high rank; surely he had few complaints.

"Especially mine."

"What're the downsides o' your job?" she couldn't help but ask.

In the silence, the ground crunched beneath their boots.

After a moment, he said, "If I fail at my work, people die. If I succeed... people die."

Her chest tightened. She understood. All too well.

"We do what we must," she said.

"Yes."

The glance he gave her made her feel more transparent than ever. Something was shifting inside her, an awareness she'd never felt before. A sensation intangible and cataclysmic. She realized that they were nearing their destination. Their conversation would soon end. After that, she'd never speak to this man again.

On impulse, she said, "If you weren't an officer, what would you be, sir?"

He stopped, pivoted to face her. "Do you know," he said in a strange voice, "no one has ever asked me that before?"

She instantly regretted her error. "Ain't my business, don't mean to pry—"

"A husband and father," he said.

Those four words, laced with quiet desire, hung between them like a garland of smoke. Clouds parted, revealing a velvet sky dizzy with diamonds, yet to Pandora, the glitter in his eyes was even more brilliant because she had never met a man like him in her entire life and was certain she never again would.

He was a true gentleman. One whose inner fire wasn't sparked by ambition or fame or fortune, but something different altogether. What Harrington, Britannia's much-heralded hero, fought and yearned for was... a family.

He wanted a wife and children of his own. A family that he would provide for, protect, and—she knew it in the deepest depths of her soul—*love*. That was what beat in the heart of this man.

She became aware of her wildly thrumming pulse. His scent curled in her nostrils, his jacket warming her from inside out. She swayed a little closer toward him, his hard face and sad eyes—

"Lieutenant-Colonel Harrington! Sir!" A panting voice, pounding footsteps.

The skeins of the moment snapped.

"What is it?" Harrington said alertly to the approaching soldier.

"'Tis Major Starky, sir. He was found in his tent. Doctor's looking at him, says his heart gave out—"

"Let's go." Harrington started off, then turned to look at her. "Miss Brown?"

Pandora's heart was racing now for an entirely different reason than just moments before. She prayed the breathlessness in her voice didn't give her away. "Yes, sir?"

"Merry Christmas."

The briefest smile touched his lips, yet it was enough. Far too much. She remained for a few precious seconds longer, watching him disappear into the night.

"Merry Christmas, Marcus Harrington," she whispered.

Then she, too, vanished into the darkness.

2

LONDON, SEPTEMBER 1829

Marcus awakened fully alert, a habit from his days in the army. Another part of him was also standing at attention, but that had nothing to do with his military past and everything to do with the gorgeous woman curled on her side next to him. His wife. His lucky Penny, who'd changed his fortunes from the moment he'd first met her at a ball. Twelve years of marriage and three strapping sons later, his desire for her had only deepened. Like a fine wine, the passion between them had grown richer, more robust and satisfying with time.

Leaning up on his elbow, he admired her sleeping profile. Her lashes were lush black fans against her alabaster cheeks, her sultry features soft and sweetly relaxed. A sound escaped from her rosy lips: half-sigh, half-moan, it was as adorable as it was tempting. When she shifted in her sleep, her plush backside nudging his cockstand, he could resist no longer.

Gently pulling the heavy raven tresses off her neck, he nuzzled the curve of her shoulder. He inhaled the fragrance of her sleep-warmed skin: jasmine and neroli, her signature scent and a potent aphrodisiac to his senses. His lips skimmed along her smooth white shoulder, his hand roving under the covers. Blood pumped through his veins as he palmed one rounded breast, savoring its firmness and silken heft.

Gently, he rolled her nipple between his thumb and forefinger. She was still asleep, but her breathing changed, the cadence quickening, the surges more shallow. Smiling to himself, he played some more, drawing the covers down so that he could see what he was doing. The sight of those luscious tits, their blushing tips hard and saucy against his fingers, threw kindling onto his fire.

His hand followed the sweet dip of her waist to the even sweeter flare of her hip. God love his wife's curvaceous figure. And the fact that, over the years, he'd won her over to the habit of sleeping in the buff... although he had a hunch that she was no longer sleeping. As he kissed her ear, his caress slid farther down to one of his favorite places of all.

Satisfaction poured through him. Just as he'd suspected.

She was wet, hot, and ready for him.

"Good morning to you, too."

Her throaty words, uttered with her eyes still closed, made him grin.

"And it's about to get better," he murmured.

"Confident, are you, Lord Blackwood?"

"Let's just say you're rather a sure thing, Lady Blackwood."

"*Someone* has a big head."

"As a matter of fact, yes." He slid his erection against the cleft of her bottom, the blunt tip prodding the soft base of her spine. "Very big, as it were."

"*Marcus.*"

But since she was giggling and her pussy, which he'd been petting all the while, had gotten wetter and hotter, he didn't take her admonition to heart. He knew his Penny, and she liked her games. He liked them, too.

He ran a possessive hand down her silky leg, pulling it back over his. With both of them laying on their sides, this position presented rather intriguing prospects. Never a man to waste a good opportunity, he positioned his shaft and thrust home.

Ah, Christ. So good. Always so good.

"Penny," he groaned.

Her reply was a breathy mangling of his name. He didn't need further encouragement. Holding her steady by the hip, he drove himself into her lush passage, deep and deeper, the fit snug and bloody perfect. He played with her pearl, circling and rubbing, pressing that sensitive little knot against his stroking cock in a way guaranteed to drive his lady wild. Moaning, she bucked wantonly against him, and he held on, not wanting this pleasure to end, not just yet.

Gritting his teeth, he kept his pace measured. Waited for her crescendo, her hitched breaths and the flush on her jiggling breasts betraying that she was nearly at her peak. *Thank God.* Gasping, she threw her head back to look at him, her stunning violet eyes bright with love and passion, and in that moment the truth reverberated within him.

I have everything. Everything I've ever wanted.

His thoughts vaporized in the blaze of their kiss. In the love and lust of their tangling tongues, their joining bodies. Only when he felt her climax did he let go. He hilted himself and held, burying his groans in his wife's hair as her rippling sheath pulled joy from him, their shared heat melding them as one.

3

Sipping chocolate, Lady Pandora Blackwood—Penny to her husband—was sorting through a pile of invitations at the breakfast table. It was an ordinary event, but she had a newfound appreciation for routine. This moment marked the passing of an all too recent danger: four months ago, an enemy had risen from her past. The once notorious spy who called himself the Spectre had reemerged to threaten her and her former colleagues. After months of blackmail and threats, the bastard had attacked her ex-comrade, Gabriel Ridgley, the Marquess of Tremont.

Tremont had dispatched the villain.

With the Spectre gone, the world was made safer—and Penny's secrets would remain where they belonged. In the past. Locked away where they couldn't harm the ones she loved.

She breathed a silent sigh of gratitude and relief before sliding a glance at her husband.

Seated to her right, Marcus was reviewing his business correspondence while he drank his coffee. One of the things she adored about him—and there were admittedly many—was the fact that he was so proper on the outside. A perfect gentleman whose style was marked by restraint. Sometimes, he erred too much in that direction, and it took plotting between her and his valet Gibson to ensure that he didn't wind up looking downright funereal.

Under Gibson's tutelage, she'd learned that the art of men's dressing lay in the details. Thus, she made sure that fine cufflinks, cravat pins, and other stylish accoutrements found their way into her husband's wardrobe on a regular basis. Gibson, for his part, employed those items to stark yet superb effect when grooming Marcus.

One of Penny's secret pleasures was knowing that beneath the plain, crisp linen and somber waistcoat lay a virile and hot-blooded man, a husband who, after a dozen years of marriage, still liked to awaken her in the manner of a randy newlywed...

Marcus set down his cup, the slight furrow between his dark brows conveying his concentration on the task at hand. Her heart fluttered as she watched him. From the moment they'd met, her soul had recognized him as hers, and the intervening years had only heightened her attraction to him.

At forty-one, Marcus was even more compelling to her senses than he'd been at five-and-twenty. He'd grown leaner, harder, the threading of grey in his thick, dark bronze hair adding to his distinguished air. His hawkish features might not be classically handsome, but their fierceness spoke of integrity and authority. The strength of moral character that had made him a military hero. In fact, his visage might have been described as overly harsh were it not for the subtle laugh lines around his eyes and mouth— lines, she liked to think, that she and their three sons had contributed to.

Marcus' gaze suddenly shifted to her; the smile in those steel blue depths made her sex quiver. He reached over and gave her hand a husbandly squeeze. He returned to opening his letters while her heart continued to pound like that of a silly debutante.

As Lady Pandora Blackwood, she'd worked diligently to build her reputation. Invitations to her soirees and balls were the most sought-after in all the *ton*. Society wags had decreed her one of the most sophisticated and glamorous hostesses in the Top Ten Thousand. Everyone knew she and Marcus had a love match, but what would they say if they knew how intemperate her feelings for him were beneath her urbane surface? How madly she loved him? How one touch from him made her want to climb astride him at the breakfast table, never mind the servants who could come in at any moment, and beg him to take her then and there?

He made love to you just an hour ago, you greedy wanton.

Her cheeks warmed. Other parts, too.

She went back to the invitations even as naughty images danced through her head. She and Marcus shared a passionate marriage bed—this morning being a case in point—but certain lines should not be crossed. She'd dedicated the last dozen years to making herself into the kind of wife that Marcus wanted. To becoming his ideal, his every fantasy. While ardor was all well and good, a man like Marcus also needed a wife who was a lady.

It was Miss Pandora Hudson, only daughter of Mr. and Mrs. Harry Hudson, of the Devonshire Hudsons, that he'd fallen in love with, after all. That was who he'd proposed to and married. Not Pandora Smith, former secret agent and bastard daughter of a whore.

As Lady Pandora, she'd made her husband happy. She would continue to make him happy. To do that, she would act like the lady she'd become... or at least save her carnal impulses for bedtime.

"What the devil?"

Marcus' oath startled her as did the clattering of his letter opener against his breakfast plate. Her gaze flew to him; never before had she seen such an expression on his face. Typically, he was a man of composure, yet now his eyes blazed with rage. A letter was clenched in his fist; throwing it down, he shoved away from the table and rose abruptly to his feet. He stood, glowering at the offending piece of paper.

"What is it?" she said in surprise.

"I'll have the hide of the bounder who wrote this," Marcus vowed grimly. "I'll hunt him down, and, by Jove, he'll answer for this slander. By the time I'm done with him, he'll wish he'd never been born—"

"What *are* you talking about, my love?" She reached over and plucked up the crumpled missive. She smoothed it out—and her throat closed.

Handwriting she'd never forget. Words that ripped the veil from her world.

The Spectre, she thought numbly. *Getting his revenge from the grave.*

"Penny?"

She turned her dazed eyes up to her husband.

"Do you know who is responsible for this defamation?" he demanded.

"I... I..." Ugly heat scalded her insides. For some reason, she couldn't get her brain to work. 'Twas as if her mental cogs were rusted into place.

"It matters not, my love. I'll find out." The muscles of his jaw were tight, his eyes slits of steel. "Whoever the bastard is, he'll pay for this insult."

She knew that look on her husband's face: that of a crusader out for justice. Panic tumbled through her. Once Marcus set upon a course, there was no stopping him. A determination to do right was woven into the fabric of his nature. He would not relent until he found his answers. The Spectre might be dead, but if Marcus went searching into the dark alleys of her past, who knew what deadly skeletons he might dig up? What dangers might befall him?

"No," she blurted. "You can't."

"Of course I can. And I will," he said curtly. "No one slanders my wife and gets away with it."

Think of something. Amongst espionage circles, she'd once been infamous for her skill at disguise and deception, yet as her husband's gaze held hers, her mind churned in desperate confusion. It refused to come up with more lies, ways to bluff her way out of disaster. For the first time, her survival instincts abandoned her.

Icy perspiration trickled beneath her bodice. As she wetted her lips, telltale heat spread over her cheeks.

"What is the matter, love? Do you know who wrote this slander..." As Marcus watched her, something shifted in his expression. Disbelief strained his voice as he said, "It *is* slander, isn't it?"

Still, she couldn't speak. Couldn't force her lips to shape the word, just one more lie, to save herself from certain destruction. Here, she was facing the deadliest opponent of them all—the truth—and she was suddenly, inexplicably out of bullets. She couldn't hold his gaze, so intense and piercing.

Familiar callused fingers tipped her chin up. "Look at me."

She did, staring into her beloved's eyes, and, to her horror, her vision began to swim. She could count on two hands the times that she'd cried in front of her husband. Being rather hotheaded by nature, she was more apt to instigate an out-and-out row than succumb to tears. He liked to tease her that, with her temperament, she would have been one of the rowdy troublemakers in his battalion. He never knew how close he'd come to the truth. Perhaps she ought to have hidden her natural tendencies, but it had been too much trouble to cultivate the art of being a watering pot, even for him.

Now, however, she couldn't stop the moisture leaking from her eyes.

"What the devil?" Marcus' tone permeated her shock.

"You mustn't pursue this. The writer of the note—he's dead," she said in a rush. "He was a spy, working for the French, and he's no longer a threat. All of this is in the past. Please I can explain—"

"The letter says you were a spy, Pandora." Her husband stared at her. "Is this true?"

Blooming hell. She fumbled for a response. "There's a good explanation—"

"It's a yes or no question," he said incredulously.

Say no. Say no. Say no.

She seemed to have lost any ability to control herself. 'Twas as if she'd let go of tightly held reins all at once, and she was flying, flying into an abyss. Terrified, she couldn't stop more tears from spilling over. Nor her chin from dipping in an infinitesimally small nod.

The silence was punctuated by sounds of domesticity beyond the room. Maids cleaning, silverware rattling on a tray. Everyday noises that seemed to come from a world away.

"And the rest of the letter?" The pain in her husband's voice serrated her insides. "It claims that you... you seduced these three men. Pierre Chenet. Jean-Philippe Martin. Vincent Barone."

The names tore into her like shrapnel. The last, in particular, left a gaping hole out of which her nightmares oozed. The alleyway of crushed violets. Smell of garbage. The taste of fear, tinny and acid, filled her mouth.

She couldn't breathe, couldn't hold Marcus' blazing gaze. "I... I..."

"Goddamnit, you will look at me and give me the truth."

She forced her eyes up. His face was now tightly controlled, wiped of expression. He wasn't her Marcus any longer; he was Lieutenant-Colonel Harrington, a man who held those in his command to the strictest levels of moral behavior. Who was now looking at his wife as he would a soldier placed on court-martial.

She'd fought too many battles not to know defeat when she saw it. No weapons left, no place to hide. *Damn the Spectre for doing this. Damn him for destroying everything.*

"I had no choice," she said through the constriction of her throat. "It was part of the mission. Please, I can explain—"

"*Explain?* How do you explain that you were a spy? A damned *whore?*"

His words sliced through her; shame bled out.

"I did... I did what I had to do," she whispered.

"You *had* to lie to me? In twelve years, not once have you mentioned that you were involved in this filthy business. *Damnation.*" He dragged his hands through his hair, his expression going from angry to ravaged. "On our wedding night, you acted like you were a virgin. Was that... was that just an act?"

"I'm sorry," she said, her voice cracking. "I didn't mean to—"

"There was *blood on the sheets*. How did it get there?" he roared.

A tremor travelled through her. In all their years together, Marcus had never raised his voice at her. But she was stripped bare now; there was nothing left to yield but the truth.

"It was chicken blood," she whispered.

Blue flames leapt in his eyes, and then he was looking at her as if she were something he'd scraped off his shoe. As if he were seeing her for the first time—and what he saw disgusted him. She didn't blame him. Even as self-revulsion made her stomach roil, she stumbled to her feet, held out a pleading hand.

"I was wrong to deceive you, Marcus. What I did was unforgivable. But I did all of it because I loved you so much—"

"*Love?*" Never had the word sounded ugly coming from his lips, but now it cracked like a whip. "Pandora—if that is even your name—you don't know what love is. If you did, you would not have betrayed me from the moment we met."

She'd faced death more than once, and yet her fear now made all past experiences fade to nothingness. Terror filled her lungs, closed over her head, waves and waves of it. Frantically, she fought to stay afloat.

"We've been happy. All I've ever wanted was to make you happy." Tears streaming down her face, she touched his sleeve. "Please, Marcus, I can make things right—"

He shook her off as if her very touch disgusted him.

"Don't," he clipped out. "It's too late."

"T-too late?" Her voice quivered.

"Our marriage is a lie. All of it. Nothing was real."

His cold, flat words punched harder than any fist. Shaking her head in denial, she said, "No, that's not true. I love you. And the children—"

"I will decide what to tell them—once I decide what to do with you."

Dread squeezed her lungs. She couldn't breathe.

He turned and headed toward the door.

"Wait," she croaked. "Where are you going?"

"That is none of your business." He spoke with his back to her. "From now on, nothing I do concerns you."

The door slammed behind him.

Alone, her strength left her. She sank to her knees, and everything she'd held back came rushing to the fore. The torrents swept over her, and for once in her life, she was lost.

❧ 4 ❧

Marcus Harrington leaned on the balcony railing and, for the first time that evening, breathed freely. The night air was cool and carried the budding scents of spring. Although lofty Mayfair rooftops crowded all around him, at least here he could see the sky, which calmed his inner restlessness. He slid a finger under his collar, loosening the life-threatening grip of his fashionable cravat. The roar of a ball in full swing seeped through the glass panes of the double doors, even though he'd closed them for privacy. He'd wanted a moment away from the mayhem. From the relentless, monotonous blur of gaiety.

Funny how he'd spent more than a decade of his life in army camps and barracks and during those last years all he'd wanted was to be back in civilization. To be away from the horrors of the battlefield. And now, two years after Waterloo, he *was* back. For good. He'd sold his commission when his older brother James died, leaving him the title.

Grief panged. Marcus had seen more than his fair share of death, and, even so, witnessing James struggle with that wasting disease, an invisible opponent that had worn his strong, vital brother down to skin and bones and then even less, had been devastating. If life was fair, James ought to still be alive, still the Marquess of Blackwood, standing where Marcus was.

But life wasn't fair.

Thus, James had been buried in the cold earth for over a year now while Marcus wore the title like an ill-fitting castoff. He'd never had his brother's charismatic personality, hadn't been groomed to be a lord, and the years fighting abroad had made him even less suited to be a marquess. What he'd thought would be a homecoming turned out to be yet another foray into foreign territory.

He was a military man: he had no idea how to carry on as a nobleman. He had no penchant for the activities that made up a fashionable life. As far as he was concerned, clothing was to keep one warm and covered without getting in one's way, and gambling and drinking to excess were a waste of time and money. Doing social rounds and making idle chitchat held even less appeal, and he hadn't the faintest clue what to do with the townhouse and coterie of servants he'd inherited.

That's why you need a wife, my boy—to help you settle into a routine, his mama had said. Despite her grief over her eldest, she roused herself from mourning to give Marcus a lecture at every opportunity. *Miss Pilkington is perfect for you. Good ton, pretty as she can stare, and an heiress to boot. You can't do better. What are you waiting for?*

He supposed his mother was right. Cora Pilkington, daughter of the evening's hosts, *was* an ideal candidate. Blonde and demure, she had perfect manners and a spotless reputation, earning her the status of a Diamond of the First Water. During their chaperoned visits, she'd proved to be charming company... if a bit overzealous in her admiration of his wartime actions. He'd proceeded with a slow, cautious courtship over the past three months, and her father, Charles Pilkington III, had made clear that an offer from Marcus would be heartily accepted.

All Marcus had to do was take that final step. Society thought the marriage a *fait accompli* already, and he didn't know why he balked. He was no rake, attached to fantasies of bachelorhood. No, he wanted to be married and to start a nursery. Cora was the rational choice. And if the idea of marrying her failed to stir elation in him... well, that had to be his own failing, not hers.

His brother wouldn't have been ruled by sentiment. A lord down to his very bones, James had always known his duty and done the right thing. If he'd concluded that Cora would make a perfect Marchioness of Blackwood, he would have married her forthwith.

As their mama would put it, *No use shilly-shallying about.*

Marcus resolved to talk to Miss Pilkington's father soon.

The orchestra suddenly grew in volume, voices swelling. He turned to see the double doors opening... and then a vision appeared. A woman so beautiful that longing began to throb in his chest, a hidden wound he never knew he had. His flesh and blood wound, the scar from a sniper's bullet, tautened on his left shoulder as awareness sizzled through him.

"Oh... hello," she said.

By Jove, even her voice was beautiful. Sultry, like her lustrous raven tresses, yet sweet like her rose-tinted lips. Mystery and innocence wrapped in one perfect package. When she smiled, his breath lodged in his throat.

"I'm sorry to intrude," she went on. "It seems you were here first. I was just looking for some privacy, but perhaps,"—although her tone was apologetic, her eyes sparkled with humor—"I am merely depriving you of yours?"

Stop gawking and say something, you idiot.

"The balcony is large enough to accommodate the both of us," he managed.

She rewarded him with another smile before coming to lean her gloved arms on the balustrade next to him. Her pose was relaxed and companionable, as casual as if they were two soldiers sharing a break on the battlements. Peering into the darkness, she did the most remarkable thing: closing her eyes, she leaned into the night and inhaled deeply. His blood pumped thickly at the unaffected sensuality of her actions. Moonlight shimmered over her flawless skin and the luscious bounty of her décolletage. It glinted off the sparkling threads shot through the fabric of her gown, the elegant white column an ode to her nubile form.

"Honeysuckle."

At the throaty word, he hastily yanked his gaze up from her voluptuous bottom. "Er, pardon?"

Her long, sooty lashes swept against dark, curving brows. Though the darkness obscured the precise color of her eyes, he guessed they were some rich shade—blue, maybe. There was no hiding the glimmer of amusement in them.

"Honeysuckle," she repeated. "Do you smell it?"

He blinked. He hadn't been paying attention before, but now he sniffed the air, and there it was: a sweet and subtle scent. "Yes," he said with surprise. "I do."

"There's musk rose too. And..." Her bosom rose delightfully as she inhaled again.

"Eglantine," he finished for her.

"Yes, that's it." Her smile made heat bloom in his gut. "A uniquely English combination. I've just returned from living abroad, you see, so I notice these things."

She was newly arrived in London then, which explained why he'd never met her before. It was inconceivable that he could have laid eyes on this woman and not noticed her. Questions burst into his head like a flock of birds at the crack of a gun—and belatedly, he realized he didn't even know her name. His sense of propriety had abandoned him, along with his capacity for rational thought.

"My apologies," he said, bowing. "Marcus Harrington, Marquess of Blackwood, at your service."

At her curtsy, executed with sensual grace, his temperature soared several degrees higher. What was the matter with him?

He'd known his fair share of women, yet he couldn't recall reacting this way to any member of the fair sex before. His was not an inconstant or flighty character; nonetheless, the regard he had for Miss Pilkington, whom just moments ago he'd been considering proposing to, now felt tepid at best. Like tea left overlong in the pot.

In contrast, this stranger's pull on him was as potent and visceral as a shot of whiskey. Make that a dozen shots. She was that tantalizing dream that he could never fully remember but which left him hard, hot, and sweat-glazed in the sheets.

"I know who you are, Lord Blackwood." Her lips curved. "I'm Pandora Hudson."

Her given name suited her. Different, exotic, the promise of the sweetest trouble. Her surname rang a bell too, although he couldn't quite place it.

"A pleasure, Miss Hudson." He bent over her hand. The contact with her slim gloved fingers sent a jolt of desire through him. *Devil and damn, get a control of yourself, man.* "Er, shall I return you to your chaperone for a proper introduction?"

"A few minutes won't matter. Seeing as I just went through the trouble of evading her," Miss Hudson said, "I think I deserve some well-earned peace, don't you?"

He couldn't argue with that. Nor with the prospect of extending what felt like a stolen, magical moment. When she returned to her earlier pose, leaning her elbows on the balustrade and looking out into the dark gardens, he did the same.

"You are not enjoying the ball?" he said.

"It's no different from any other. A crush is a crush." Her creamy shoulders moved in a careless shrug. "The truth is they always make me feel rather lonely."

He couldn't fathom Miss Pandora Hudson being left alone at any ball. Or anywhere, for that matter. Unless all the gentlemen in the world had suddenly gone deaf and blind and stupid besides.

"I can't imagine there's a single empty line on your dance card," he said sincerely.

"That's true." She slid him a look. Not coy, but assessing. "I didn't say I was alone—just lonely. One has little to do with the other, wouldn't you agree?"

Her astute words triggered a strange recognition in him. A sense of familiarity... which of course made no sense. With each passing moment, he knew he would never forget a female such as this.

"Where did you say you lived abroad?" he said on impulse.

"I didn't." Her eyes held a hint of laughter. "But the answer is this: nowhere and everywhere. My parents spent their time travelling the Continent, and I was raised in different finishing schools along the way. France, Switzerland, Italy—toss a coin on a map, and chances are I've lived where it lands."

Her description triggered Marcus' recollection of her parents. Although he'd never met the Hudsons personally, he knew them by name. They'd been good *ton*, a society couple who'd lived abroad as the husband had a fancy for digging up relics and old bones.

"An unusual upbringing," he commented. "What brings you back?"

"My parents died. I'm alone in the world,"—shadows flitted across her fine features—"and I wanted to see where they came from. Where *I* came from, I suppose. In essence? I wanted to find a place where I belong."

That this exquisite creature should harbor any doubt about her place in the world both baffled and entranced him. She possessed a natural confidence as if she'd seen much of life despite her young age... and yet there was a hint of vulnerability in her wistful tone. A longing that held a mirror up to his own, causing the ache in his chest to grow. Her rare blend of qualities also roused all his protective instincts.

"I'm sure you'd belong anywhere you want to," he said firmly.

She studied him a moment. "Is the same true for you, Lord Blackwood?"

"For me?"

"Well, yes. I can't help but notice that there's a roomful of people in there," —her head tipped in the direction of the balcony doors—"eager to celebrate your wartime heroics. And yet here you are with me."

"Is my desire for escape so obvious?" he said ruefully.

"Only to a fellow balcony refugee."

He laughed. "Damn, but you're a breath of fresh air, Miss Hudson. I wish I'd met you inside. Then I wouldn't have had to seek out this balcony in the first place."

"Society can be stifling. I imagine especially for a man like you."

"A man like me?" He quirked a brow.

"A soldier. A man of action," she said matter-of-factly. "Compared to life or death on the battlefield, the *ton* must surely seem frivolous."

He stared at her in astonishment. Somehow she'd plucked his thoughts straight out of his head.

"Tell me, Miss Hudson, is mind reading a skill they teach at finishing schools for ladies abroad?"

"I wish. Then at least I would have a ladylike accomplishment to boast of."

"Never say you have no accomplishments. I wouldn't believe it."

"Let's just say my talents aren't precisely fit for the drawing room." Mischief danced in her eyes. "I couldn't sew a straight seam to save my life. And you'd be running for yours if you heard me on the pianoforte."

Grinning, he said, "It can't be all that bad."

"Trust me. It is." Her nose wrinkled, and even that was adorable. "I shan't make an ordinary wife, that's for certain."

The thought hit him with the ferocity of a cannonball.

"Are you attached?" The words rushed from him.

She regarded him solemnly. God, her eyes—temptation itself. "Not yet."

"Good." He released a breath. "Miss Hudson, I know this may seem forward and I swear to you I'm not an impetuous chap by nature, but I'd like to call on you. With your permission, of course."

"You have it." She smiled at him. Straightening from the railing, she turned.

"Wait. You're leaving?"

"My reputation, remember?"

"But when can I call? Where?" he called after her.

She paused at the doors, her lips shaped in a knowing curve. "I have a feeling that you'll figure it out. It was a pleasure, my lord. Adieu."

"Good night," he replied.

He watched her goddess-like form disappear through the doors and then turned back to the garden. Luckily, no one was there to see him—because he was grinning like a fool. He couldn't help it. Because now he *knew* what he wanted, what his life had been missing all along.

Placing his hands on the cool stone, he looked out into the universe and, damn, if Miss Pandora Hudson hadn't changed it for him. The world was no longer colorless or bleak. Surrounded by the dazzling night sky and blossoming spring garden, he saw his future in vivid, breathtaking color.

And he couldn't wait.

$\text{❧}\quad 5 \quad\text{❧}$

SEPTEMBER 1829

When two days and nights of drinking at his club did nothing to diminish his rage, Marcus left Town. He was beginning to incur the curiosity of other club members—and God knew White's was populated by some of the worst damned gossips in all of London. Besides, putting distance between him and the treacherous harlot to whom he'd given his name was the best course of action. He wasn't a man quick to temper but, by Jove, he was afraid of what he might do if he saw her. All those years... all those *lies*.

Nothing between them real, nothing true.

Pierre Chenet. Jean-Philippe Martin. Vincent Barone.

The names clawed at his chest, red seeping into his vision, and he spurred his horse on, riding as if he were trying to outrun Satan himself—or, more accurately, a she-devil whose vows of love had been nothing more than the most venomous deception...

Past nightfall, he found himself at his old friend's hunting lodge near Winchester. There were few whose company Marcus would seek out at the moment; Richard Murray, Viscount

Carlisle, was one of them. Although they hadn't seen each other for almost a year—the viscount preferred country life over town life—Carlisle could always be counted on for a night of drinking and playing billiards with minimal conversation necessary (if they did talk, it would be about good, solid topics such as horses and business). If that didn't prove enough of a distraction, they could always go outside and shoot things. An avid sportsman, Carlisle kept his grounds well-stocked with game.

Marcus' hopes for the evening began to fade, however, as he was shown into the manor by a surly butler. Despite his own unsettled state, he saw with some shock the changes that had taken place since he'd been here last. He passed bare walls, their paper peeling, and an entire room stripped of furniture. When he arrived at the study, his worst suspicions were confirmed.

The cabinets were empty, stripped of Carlisle's extensive rifle collection. The billiards table was gone. Even the paintings of classic hunting scenes had disappeared. In the dim, barren space, about the only thing that remained was a pair of battered wingchairs and side tables set next to the fire.

Carlisle rose from one of them. The Scot was a tall fellow, dark-haired with saturnine features. "Blackwood, welcome." He raised a brow. "I wasn't expecting you."

"Yes, sorry. I ought to have sent word. If it's a bad time—"

"Nonsense. Come sit. We'll have a drink," Carlisle said.

Once they were both settled in the wingchairs, whiskies in hand, Marcus addressed the situation. "How bad are things?" he said quietly.

"They're not ideal at the moment." Carlisle took a drink.

The Scot was the king of understatement. In fact, his sardonic wit coupled with an intensely private nature had earned him a reputation for being standoffish. Marcus, however, had known the other for the better part of a decade and, when it came down to it, couldn't name a more honorable gentleman. It was a little known fact that Carlisle had inherited a financial disaster, and he'd taken on the Sisyphean task of reversing the family fortune. He rarely spoke of it and never complained. Just dealt with one crisis after another and carried on.

He was the kind of man you'd want at your back in battle—and that wasn't a compliment Marcus gave easily. Still, the viscount could be hard-headed and prickly when it came to his pride, as likely to welcome assistance as he would a bullet to the brain.

Nonetheless, Marcus had to try. Leaning forward, he said, "If there's anything I can do to help—"

"I've got it in hand."

Typical Carlisle.

"Unfortunately," the Scot went on, "our options for the evening are rather limited. This,"—he pointed at the whiskey bottle—"will be our main entertainment, I'm afraid."

Marcus downed the contents of his glass. It didn't drown out his demons: hell, there wasn't enough whiskey in the world to do that. Just like that, his rage broke the surface.

It was bad enough that Pandora had been a spy. Like most Englishmen, he viewed espionage with distrust and not a little disdain. It was a dishonorable activity—a necessary evil, perhaps, but evil nonetheless. To think that the woman he'd married had been involved in such disgraceful business... he could scarcely credit it. Didn't *want* to.

Even worse, he had to confront the fact that his wife—*his Penny*—had given herself freely before their marriage. Had used her body to play despicable games and then *pretended* to be a virgin on their wedding night. Acid scalded his gut as the memory surfaced of their wedding trip at his cottage in the Cotswolds.

The morning after their first night together, he'd just returned from washing up. Penny was puttering behind the dressing screen, and he sat on the bed, waiting for her. Marveling at the passion that had nigh set his marital bed aflame—and wondering if his new bride might be up for another tumble before breakfast. But then his gaze caught on the stains: large reddish-brown splotches amidst the rumpled sheets. Remorse struck him like a thunderbolt.

"Marcus, is that you? I was thinking that after breakfast we might take a walk..." Penny rounded the screen, stopping as her gaze met his. "Whatever is the matter? You look like you've seen a ghost."

He went to her, taking her hand and bringing it to his lips.

"Forgive me, my love," he muttered.

"Forgive you? Whatever for?"

For being a selfish ass. For not realizing that my pleasure meant your pain.

"I hurt you." Self-loathing roughened his voice. "I'm sorry, Penny. I never meant to."

"Hurt me? Oh..." Her lashes lowered. She bit her lip. "It wasn't that bad. Truly."

"I don't want it to be bad at all. You know that, don't you?" He tipped her chin up, relief and tenderness bursting in his chest at the love and trust he saw in her violet eyes. Thank *God* his carelessness hadn't damaged her faith in him. Humbled, he vowed, "I swear it'll get better. I'll make it better for you."

She smiled at him, and he didn't know how she could after he'd been such a brute—so consumed by his own desire that he hadn't sensed that she must have been hurting. In truth, he'd believed that she'd enjoyed their lovemaking every bit as much as he had, those little moans she'd made, the sweet bite of her nails against his back—

"No time like the present, darling." She stunned him by rising on her toes, putting her arms around his neck, and whispering in his ear, "There's plenty of time before breakfast."

The memory faded, but this time it wasn't poignant gratitude that it left in its wake but a bitterness that wouldn't recede. Bile lingered in his throat, his hands clenching around the arms of the chair.

I adored you, thought you were my soulmate. Damn you for deceiving me. For making me the world's biggest dupe.

"What is the matter with you, Blackwood?"

Carlisle's words punctured his silent seething.

He pulled air into his lungs. "Nothing."

"You look like you swallowed glass."

"I'm tired. It was a long ride," he said curtly.

"Which you took on horseback, without valet or belongings. No protection either—even with the risk of highwaymen lurking about."

Perhaps he ought to have gone somewhere more welcoming. Perdition, for example.

"Never known you to pry," he said, his jaw taut.

"Never known you to arrive unannounced on my doorstep looking like something the cat dragged in."

"Thank you for your hospitality." Marcus shoved up from his chair. "I'll be on my way—"

"Don't be a damned fool. Sit. If you don't want to talk, fine."

"Fine." Marcus returned his arse to the seat, staring moodily into the flames.

After a moment, his host said, "How's the lovely Lady Blackwood?"

"Devil take you, Carlisle."

"Probably." The viscount raised an inquisitive brow.

With his elbows on his knees, Marcus dragged his hands through his hair, tugging at his scalp. Suddenly, it was all too much for his alcohol-infused and sleep-deprived brain to contain.

"I've left her," he blurted.

"Ah." Carlisle didn't sound too surprised. "Any particular reason?"

She was a bloody spy. Slept with three men that I know of. Lied to me —about everything... God, was our marriage a mere cover? A way for her to hide from her past?

His mind reeled, his gust twisting at the possibilities, all of them ugly. "Our relationship is based on a lie," he said starkly.

"That's marriage for you. Fidelity, death-do-us-part, promises to obey." The other's mouth had a cynical edge. "All vows meant to be broken."

In his early thirties, Carlisle remained a stalwart bachelor.

"It's worse than that." Through the haze of anger and alcohol, Marcus nonetheless found that he couldn't betray the truth of Pandora's past. He couldn't betray *her*—that was rich. The fact that he still felt protective of her only made him more furious. "I won't get into the details of it, but she wed me under false pretenses. And everything since—our lives, our home, our *children*." His voice hoarsened as he thought of his sons. Dear God, how were they going to be affected by all of this? "All of it was conceived from a lie."

"Fruit of the poisonous tree?"

He gave a rough nod. Taking the bottle Carlisle silently handed him, he refilled his glass and tossed back the drink. He had a glimpse of the chaos, the churning devastation beneath the waves of rage, and he... he couldn't go there. Couldn't contemplate the reality that his marriage—his entire *life* as he knew it—was no more than a falsehood. A mirage of such joy that agony speared him at the thought of losing it.

But he couldn't lose it, could he?

Because he'd never had it in the first place.

He downed the liquid, the burn nothing compared to his inner inferno.

"What are you going to do?" Carlisle said.

In answer, Marcus sloshed more liquor into his glass.

"Are you planning on taking legal action?" his friend prodded.

His jaw clenched. On his ride over, crazed thoughts had whipped through his mind, and they'd included legal remedies that were within his right to pursue. Seeing as Pandora had wed him under fraudulent pretenses, he could seek an annulment...

but any offspring of an annulled marriage would become illegitimate. His sons would lose their status and their inheritance.
Under no circumstances would he do that to them.

That left divorce. This option was only marginally better. The
scandal that would ensue would taint all of his family—including
the boys—forever.

In the best scenario, they'd all become fodder for gossip, a
laughingstock; in the worst, his family would become social pari-
ahs. And for what? So that he could get retribution? His pound of
flesh? His temples pounded with the truth: there *was* no remedy
for what Pandora had done to him.

She'd ripped his heart out, drawn and quartered his very soul.

"I don't know what I'm going to do." He swigged the rest of
his spirits.

"From where I'm sitting, you have two options. End your
marriage—or learn to live with it." Carlisle paused, cocking his
head. "Did she tell you why she did it?"

"Why she did what?"

"Lied to you."

"I didn't ask," he snapped. "It was enough that she did—for
twelve bloody years."

Carlisle raised his brows. "Point taken. In my experience,
however, having full possession of the facts aids the rendering of
any decision. Up to you, of course. You're welcome to mull over
matters here as long as you like."

Marcus jerked his chin in sullen thanks.

"I've just remembered. I've got a deck of cards lying about
somewhere. How about a game?"

"Capital." Anything was better than continuing the
conversation.

As Carlisle hunted for the elusive deck, Marcus rubbed his
temples, willing the pounding to stop. Somehow he'd have to find
a way to lock down his emotions—his rage in particular—so that
he could think clearly about the future. It struck him that never

before in his life had he had difficulty making calm, rational decisions. During the war, he'd been known for having a cool head and
ice in his veins during the most catastrophic of situations.

Hell, twice in his life he'd come within Death's crosshairs. In
Toulouse, during the capture and securing of critical enemy
ground, a sniper's bullet had sliced through his left shoulder. Had
the enemy's aim been true, he'd be dead. Same thing near Quatre
Bras, only that time the shot had whizzed right by his ear.

Both times he'd been mere inches from losing his life... and
when those moments had passed and he'd found himself still
breathing, he'd picked himself up and soldiered on. It was what he
did—who he was.

Never before had he lost that will to carry on. To confront
reality and do what had to be done. Anguish festered around the
pain. *Damn you, Penny. Damn you for that as well.*

Carlisle dragged his chair over and set a tattered pack on the
side table.

"Do you want to deal or shall I?" the Scot said.

"It doesn't matter," Marcus said dully.

Thanks to his wife's perfidy, nothing did. Not any longer.

🐝 6 🐝

"Papa's home!"

At her youngest son Owen's happy shout, butterflies swarmed in Pandora's belly. She forced a smile. "Yes, dearest. Now come here and let me fix your hair. You don't want Papa to see you looking like you've just been in a wrestling match, do you?"

Not one to hold still, her five-year-old son squirmed as she attempted to smooth down his wild mop of ebony curls. In appearance and manner, he took after her.

"Ethan was wrestling too," Owen pointed out.

"Yes, but I won," Ethan said loftily. Her middle child had her eyes and Marcus' gilded brown hair. "And I didn't have to muss up my hair doing so."

"You didn't win! I only stopped wrestling because I heard Papa's carriage—"

"Quiet, you two." The imperious command came from her eldest son James. At eleven, Jamie had his father's serious mien and a tall, gangly build that would one day be as muscular as his sire's. "Papa has been gone a fortnight on important business. He shan't want to be greeted with pandemonium on the home front," he advised his brothers.

Shame and gratitude tightened Pandora's throat as she thought of Marcus' letter to the boys. Ever the good father, he'd written them with the excuse that he'd been called away on urgent business so that they wouldn't worry. So they wouldn't know the truth of what had transpired between their parents: the rift that her lies had caused.

Now he was home, and she didn't know what to expect. Didn't know if the time apart would prove her enemy or her ally. All she knew was that the two weeks of separation—the longest of their marriage—had been hell for her.

She hadn't been able to eat or sleep. For years, she hadn't had a nightmare; happiness and the security of falling asleep every night in Marcus' arms had walled off the old terror, but now it had broken through. Three times in the past fortnight, she'd awoken gasping against the leather glove, the cold stone of the alleyway against her back, the scent of crushed violets mingling with blood...

During the day, she was able to shove the memories back into the locked box where they belonged. She tried to keep up a cheerful front for the sake of the children; inside she was hollow, gutted out by an abundance of tears she hadn't known she could weep and the overwhelming terror that she'd destroyed every-thing. She still didn't understand why the truth had leaked from her like the fester from a boil... Shivering, she counted herself lucky that the worst of it hadn't emerged.

Sickly shame trickled through her. Only three others had knowledge of her most dark and despicable secret. One was her dearest confidante Flora. The second was Octavian, who'd given her the tools to put an end to her powerlessness. The third was dead and, she hoped, burning for an eternity in hell.

That part of your past is done. Focus on the future. On making things right with Marcus.

Like any good spy, she knew when the game was up and there was no longer any place to hide. She had to give her husband the truth—everything except that which would make him despise her further. She would beg his forgiveness; if he could give her another chance, she would make amends in whatever ways he would allow. There were no excuses for her deceptions. She could only explain that everything she'd done had been because she'd fallen in love with him—because she'd known that a gentleman like him could never love a woman like her in return.

Yes, she could give Marcus most of the truth. In the best case scenario, he might be able to forgive her for her lowly origins, for being a spy, perhaps even for deceiving him about her sexual experience. But if he were to discover how sullied she truly was...

Fear and self-disgust washed over her. No, he must *never* find out about that. If he did, whatever love he had for her would surely die for good then, and that was a consequence she couldn't live with.

As his familiar, precise footsteps sounded in the hallway, anticipation palpitated in her. She had the panicky wish that she'd taken more care with her toilette this morning. She knew she looked haggard from yet another restless night. If she'd known that he would be returning today, she would have applied subtle cosmetic to hide the dark circles under her eyes, the hollows beneath her cheekbones. She wished she'd worn her best morning gown, the lavender silk with the lace trim and seed pearls embroidered on the bodice—

As if paint and a dress are going to bail you out of this disaster. Don't be stupid. Focus.

The door to the drawing room opened, and Marcus walked in. Her chest squeezed at the sight of her beloved. Unlike her own appearance, his seemed to be entirely unaffected by their fortnight apart. He looked his usual handsome, austere self. The dark navy jacket and grey trousers fit his virile form like a second skin. His bronze hair gleamed in thick, orderly waves.

"Papa!" Their three sons bounded over to greet him like eager puppies.

Marcus ruffled their heads in turn, greeting them with fatherly affection. "Hello, lads. What have you been up to in the last fortnight?"

"I've been working on mathematics," Jamie said seriously, "and Mr. Johnson says I'm making very good progress with fractions."

"Excellent," Marcus said.

Jamie beamed.

Not to be outdone, Ethan said, "I memorized all the Kings and Queens of England."

"Have the memory of an elephant do you, son?" Marcus said with approval.

Ethan grinned at him.

Then, crouching to be eye level with their youngest son, Marcus said, "And you, Owen? What have you accomplished?"

Owen chewed on his lip, his brow furrowed. "I've grown... at least an inch."

Ethan snorted. "That's not an accomplishment."

"It is too!"

"It isn't. You don't have to do anything to grow—it just happens."

Owen's cherubic face flushed. "I'm going to grow bigger than *you*. Then I'm going to beat you at wrestling and—"

"Boys." Collecting herself, Pandora went over to join them. Softly, she said, "Don't beleaguer your Papa when he's only just arrived home."

Marcus rose, his gaze cutting to hers. A vise gripped her heart. The warmth with which he'd greeted their children vanished. The eyes that met hers were cold and shuttered.

"Marcus," she whispered.

"My lady."

His response, chilly and formal, raised the hairs on her skin. At home, he always called her "Pandora" or "Penny," the pet name he'd given her. In the past, he would greet her with a kiss, a touch, a gesture to show her that he'd missed her. Today, now, she was greeted with... nothing.

What did you expect? A loving welcome? Find a way to fix this.

Mindful of the children, she shaped her lips into a smile. "Boys, it's time to start your lessons. You can visit with Papa at lunch."

"But *Mama*," the boys chorused in protest.

At least the three were in agreement upon something.

"Go on, now," Marcus said. "I need to speak with your mother. I'll see you all later."

Reluctantly, their children tromped off, leaving them alone.

"We have to talk," she began.

"My study," her husband said curtly.

He turned, his back a wall to her as he led the way. She followed, her heartbeat measuring every step of the way. She sent up a desperate prayer.

God, if you can hear me, please let Marcus forgive me. I know I'm not good enough for him, but I vow I'll change—turn over a new leaf, do anything at all—to win him back.

———

Marcus closed the door, sealing himself and his wife in the dark paneled room. He'd chosen his study because of the privacy it offered and because he conducted his business affairs there. Over the past fortnight, when his anger had finally abated somewhat, he'd come to the grim conclusion that he'd been far too gullible, too soft and trusting, when it came to his marriage. He'd been so smitten with Pandora that he'd let her run roughshod over him. From now on, he needed to approach his relationship with his wife the way he did other aspects of his life: with a cool head and unwavering authority.

He wouldn't let himself be blinded by love. Not any longer.

At present, he was confronted with the unpleasant task of

discerning the truth so that he could make decisions about the future.

He went to his desk. He leaned against the front edge, his boots planted solidly as he gazed down at her. Seated in a chair facing the desk, Pandora was as beautiful and sultry as ever, but she also looked... tired. There were smudges beneath her eyes, her cheekbones more prominent as if she'd lost weight. He steeled himself against concern, against her beseeching expression.

"Marcus, you have every right to be angry at me——" she began.

"Yes, I do." It took willpower, but he managed to sound calm. "That is neither here nor there, however. The problem that lies before us is the future: that of our marriage and children."

"If you can forgive me, I promise that I'll do whatever——"

"You will be quiet and listen to me."

At his tone, her indigo eyes went wide. Good. She needn't think that she could manipulate him—as she'd apparently been doing for the entire length of their relationship. Icy fury gripped his gut. He'd no longer be her puppet, an unwitting toy in her games.

"I have questions to ask. You will answer them," he said. "Based on your answers, I will decide upon our future. By the by, if I detect so much as a hint of a lie, I will begin divorce proceedings and scandal be damned. Do I make myself clear?"

Her throat worked, her cheeks paling. "Very."

"Good. Let's begin with your name. Your true name."

"It's Pandora," she said.

At least she hadn't lied about that.

"But Hudson wasn't the name I was born with," she added in quiet tones.

Anger surged; he tamped it down. "What is your real surname?" he said coldly.

Her lashes lowered, fluttered against her creamy skin. "I don't know."

"Don't play games with me," he warned. "What do you mean you don't bloody know?"

"I mean I don't know who my parents were." Her bosom rose and fell; her eyes met his. "I was born a bastard. At the orphanage where I was raised, they told me my mother was a prostitute, and I was an unfortunate consequence of her profession. She left me there when I was a month old; I have no memory of her. Apparently, she told them she'd named me Pandora because I brought her a world of trouble." She paused. "They gave me the surname Smith at the orphanage because no one knew who my father was."

Shock percolated through Marcus. Of all the explanations he'd been expecting, it hadn't been this. He stared at his wife—the very image of a fashionable lady—and couldn't reconcile it with the past she'd just revealed. She was illegitimate... had been abandoned to an orphanage? Before he could recover, she went on.

"By the time I was ten, I was making my living as a flower girl in Covent Garden. No, that's not precisely true." Her lips pressed together before she said, "I sold flowers, but most of my earnings came from being a pickpocket."

Witnessing what he had as an officer, Marcus didn't think he could be struck speechless. Yet there he was. All capacity for speech... gone.

"I was rather good at it. Small hands, quick reflexes." Her lips tipped up, but it wasn't a smile. "Stealing kept my belly full, gave me a roof over my head at night. It wasn't the easiest life, but it wasn't the worst. Then I met Octavian."

Marcus' hands clenched the edge of the desk. He wasn't sure he wanted to hear what was coming next. Didn't like the quiver she was clearly trying to hide in her voice, the shadows gathering in her eyes.

"He was a spymaster for the Crown. He'd chanced to see me at work, and apparently I impressed him with my skills, my ability,"—her voice caught ever so slightly—"to survive. He offered me a way out of the gutter: a position on his team."

"You were *ten*," Marcus bit out.

"Close to eleven. And definitely," she said, her tone flat, "wise beyond my years."

"What business did this Octavian bounder have for a young girl?"

"At first, I mostly observed and ran errands. But Octavian was grooming me for bigger things. Given that he was a spymaster and bachelor, he couldn't look after me. So he put me under the care of a couple named Harry and Flora Hudson."

Her supposed parents, the in-laws Marcus had never met. The ones who'd apparently died and left her in a boarding school abroad.

Grimly, Marcus said, "The Hudsons were spies as well?"

She nodded. "Harry was an agent—and since Flora was devoted to her husband and refused to leave his side, she became one, too. Their good blood and Harry's interest in archaeology provided the perfect cover for their espionage work. I traveled with them, and they trained me, raised me as their own. I owe them everything." Her ivory throat rippled, her voice emerging in a whisper. "Harry was killed not long after Waterloo. A carriage accident. He'd fought so hard for peace and didn't live long enough to enjoy it. After that, Flora lost the will to go on."

Marcus' chest clenched at the sheen in Pandora's eyes. He couldn't deny that she had been through much—so much that he could scarcely fathom it. At the same time, fury surged that she'd kept this—all of it—from him. That she hadn't trusted him... that she'd betrayed the trust that he, like a great bloody fool, had given to *her* without reservation.

The galling truth was that he was weak where she was concerned. Even now, as she laid out the ignominious facts, the countless lies she'd told him, he had the inconceivable desire to take her into his arms. To tell her everything would be all right. To protect the vulnerability he'd sensed in her from the start.

He quelled the instinct and went to the window, putting distance between them. Staring out into the autumn garden, he tried to absorb some of its calm. The gilded serenity that was a universe away from his own seething turmoil.

"How long were you a spy?" he said.

"When I turned thirteen, Octavian judged me ready for missions. He gave me the code name Pompeia. I worked for him until just before I met you at the Pilkington Ball." A hesitation. "Do you remember it?"

Of course he bloody did.

"Did you engineer that meeting?" he said curtly. "Was our marriage a part of your new disguise? A way to get out of the spy business?"

"*No*. Marcus," she said, her syllables quivering, "please believe this, if nothing else: I fell in love with you from the first moment we met. I gave up espionage *because* of you. Everything I did was because I loved you so much and knew that you'd never love me back as Pandora Smith. I had to make myself a better woman for you—"

"So you lied to me because you love me?" His eyes sliced to hers. "Pretended to be a debutante—a pure and untouched *lady* to win my heart?"

Her eyes glimmered. She pressed her trembling lips together... but she didn't deny it.

For him, that was the most painful truth in all of this. He wished she might have just stabbed or shot him instead. Because the thought of any other man touching her...

"How many?" He forced out the words.

A pulse leapt in her throat. "Marcus—"

"*How many?*"

"Three," she whispered. "The ones named in the letter."

Pierre Chenet. Jean-Philippe Martin. Vincent Barone.

The names, branded on his brain, blazed red-hot. Those bastards had made love to his wife, the woman he'd believed to be exclusively his. They'd known the sweetness of Penny's kiss, the unspeakable pleasure of being inside her—

"It wasn't lovemaking." Her plea broke through his swirling vortex of agony. "It was... one time, with each of them. There was no pleasure involved—it was the opposite. Back then, I thought of it as completing a mission. It was the only life I knew. I didn't think I..."—her voice broke—"deserved any better."

He didn't want to feel empathy for her. Didn't want the maelstrom of emotion that accompanied the destruction of his world as he knew it. His much-vaunted self-control was already pushed to its very limit.

"That's enough," he snapped. "I don't want to hear another word about your sordid past."

She bit her lip but kept on talking. "The note you received was, as I said, from an old nemesis. He's dead now. My past... it can die with him." She came to him, and, stunned, he watched his urbane and glamorous wife go down on her knees in front of him. She took one of his hands in both of hers, her beautiful face turned up to his, her eyes glimmering. "I know lying about my past is unforgiveable, but since our marriage, I've been a good and true wife to you. All I've wanted is to make you happy. And we've been happy, haven't we? If you could somehow find it in your heart to give me another chance, I'll make you even happier. I'll make amends, do whatever you ask..."

"Can you change the past?" he said hoarsely.

Tears slipped from the corners of her eyes, sliding down her cheeks.

Can't think. Don't want to feel. He pulled away, rubbed his hands over his face. "I need time."

"Please, Marcus—"

"Do not push me, Pandora," he warned. "I will think on our future and decide what to do next. In the meantime, we will keep up appearances in front of the children. In public, you will play the part of mama and wife as if nothing has happened. And if you step one foot out of line, I will divorce you and to hell with the consequences. Am I understood?"

"Yes," she said in a suffocated voice. "Marcus, I love you—"

"Do not say those words to me again," he bit out. "Do I make myself clear?"

She flinched as if he'd physically struck her.

"Answer me." Goddamnit, he hated himself for being a bastard. Hated her for pushing him into acting like one.

"Yes," she whispered. "Very clear."

Furious at her—at himself—he stalked out.

7

1817

P enny had always had a temper. Octavian had cautioned her about it; Harry and Flora had taught her to control it. From the latter two—Flora especially—she'd learned to channel her hotheaded tendencies and use them to her advantage as a spy. Consequently, as Pompeia, her trademarks had been boldness and derring-do, even in the face of great odds.

As a wife, however, Penny was learning that controlling one's pique was a different matter altogether. Especially when one was married to a man as stubborn as her husband. After spending a glorious wedding trip at his cozy property in the Cotswolds, they'd returned to London. Which was when she realized that the honeymoon was over—both literally and figuratively.

Marcus returned to his routine. While he visited her bed every night and they breakfasted together, he was gone on business during the day, then off to his club after that. Occasionally, he escorted her to a social affair. Other than that, she found herself alone... *a lot*. She knew she needed her own routine, but it proved difficult to find one that didn't drive her out of her skull with boredom or irritation. Two weeks of this and she was ready to burst out of her skin.

After a lifetime of poverty and danger, one would think that having idle time and too much money to spend would be a welcome change. It wasn't. She'd rather be chased by enemy agents through the warren-like streets of the Marais than endure another visit with two-faced bitches who smiled at her politely and then wagged their forked tongues behind her back. Yet social torture and endless visits to the dressmaker seemed to be the cornerstones of the genteel female existence. Since Penny was determined to be a proper marchioness for Marcus, this would have to be her life, too.

Needless to say, this did not put her in the best of moods.

Now she turned on her bench at her vanity to face her husband. Standing in the doorway of her dressing room, he was austere perfection in his black silk dressing robe, his hair still wet and curling from his bath. Even casually dressed, he looked handsome and dignified... but that didn't make his request—or more accurately, his *decree*—any more reasonable.

"I told you before," she retorted. "I am not having supper with your mama again."

"You are. We can't avoid her forever, darling," he said.

"*You* don't have to avoid her. You can go." She crossed her arms. "And you can make excuses for me—tell her I have a megrim or that I've come down with the Plague."

Marcus' lips tipped up slightly, but he didn't relent. "I'm not going to lie for you."

"Fine. Then tell her the truth." Penny rose, her primrose satin dressing robe swirling around her. "Tell her I don't *want* to go to her supper party because she is condescending and rude. She makes no bones about disliking me, Marcus, and how much she wishes you'd wed someone else. If I have to hear one more word about the Perfect Miss Pilkington, I swear to God I shall scream."

"You're overreacting," he said—the absolutely *wrong* thing to say as far as she was concerned. "Mama is merely surprised at our marriage, as she has every right to be. It did take place with some haste."

"Marry in haste, repent in leisure?" she said bitterly. "I'm sure your mother wishes you were repenting. I hear Cora Pilkington is still free."

"There's no need to be flippant. Mama will come to accept our marriage in time. As for Miss Pilkington, she has nothing to do with this."

"She has plenty to do with it," Penny said hotly. "She's leading a dashed campaign against me."

"A campaign? How do you mean?"

The fact that Marcus looked puzzled elevated her temperature another dangerous notch. "I mean she's using her influence against me. She's making it difficult for me to enter certain circles."

"Has she been rude to you?" he said, frowning.

"Not directly." She waved a frustrated hand. "That's not the way her sort does it."

Society, Penny was learning, carried on its own version of espionage. Debutantes wielded words like stilettos, used gossip and innuendo to poison, and hid behind shining shields of virtue and politesse. To Penny, the world of the *ton* was every bit as treacherous as the world she'd inhabited before, and Cora Pilkington, the coy blond bitch, was the worst of the lot.

"How, precisely, does her *sort* do it?" her husband inquired.

It frustrated Penny to no end that she had to explain such obvious facts to his lordship. "Cora Pilkington whispers behind her fan to her cronies when I'm around. Her compliments are more false than her eyelashes. And she... she looks *smug*."

"If looking smug were a crime, the entire *ton* would be behind bars. Have you any real evidence of Miss Pilkington's plot against you?"

Fuming at his reasonable tone, Penny said, "You want an

example? Fine. At Lady Ippleby's luncheon last week, I was standing with Miss Pilkington and her friends when a spider crawled past, and Miss Pilkington screeched. Since she looked ready to faint, I stomped on the blasted thing."

"And?"

"She thanked me," Penny said darkly.

"Ah. Clearly, she has it in for you."

"Do *not* mock me. It was *how* she thanked me that showed her true character." Anger heated Penny's chest at the memory of Cora's snide, breathy tones, which she now mimicked. "*You're so hardy, Lady Blackwood, compared to the rest of us fragile blooms. I declare, I'd faint dead away if the remnants of that dreadful creature were clinging to the bottom of* my *slipper.*"

Following Cora's lead, the other hens had shivered and taken a step back from Penny as if she'd caught some miserable disease.

"That's it?" Looking exasperated, Marcus said, "Perhaps being afraid of spiders, Miss Pilkington merely admires your lack of squeamishness. Whatever the case, I'm sure she didn't mean to offend. In fact, when I saw her last, she had nothing but kind words to say about you."

God's teeth, how could he be so obtuse? How could the brilliant Lieutenant-Colonel Harrington, hero of the battlefield, be so bloody *stupid* when it came to females? Of course, that had worked to her advantage in the past... but *still*.

"It's no surprise that she'd say that to *you*. She wants you to believe that she's virtuous. All the while, she's a snake in the grass, waiting to slither into your bed," Penny said indignantly.

"That is both ridiculous and offensive." Marcus' features tightened with distaste. "Moreover, you are veering wildly off topic. We were discussing your requested presence at my mama's supper party, which has naught to do with Miss Pilkington. This is about you doing your duty as my wife—as the Marchioness of Blackwood."

"Do *not* lecture me about duty."

"Don't act like a spoiled child, and I won't have to."

At his calm superiority, her irritation boiled over. "If I'm acting like a *child*, then it's because you've assigned me to that role!"

"What the devil does that mean?"

"It means, Marcus, that when you go gallivanting off to your meetings or your club, you leave me here, alone in the house, with nothing to do," she said acidly.

"First of all, I'm not gallivanting—I'm attending to business interests." His jaw clenched. "Secondly, there's plenty for you to do."

"Such as?"

His brows lowered, his impatience now palpable. "Run the household. Receive callers. Go to the bloody dressmaker, I don't know. Whatever it is ladies do."

"For your information, it takes one hour of my day to meet with the housekeeper and the butler to ensure that the house is running smoothly. And I've *been* shopping." Her temper taking over, she stormed over to her three enormous wardrobes, flinging their doors open one by one, exposing guts of satin, silk, and chiffon. "I can't fit anything more in there."

"So buy another wardrobe," he growled.

"Excellent. So deduct an additional hour spent on Bond Street, which leaves,"—she tapped a finger against her chin—"*ten hours* a day to contend with. I repeat, what am I to do with myself?"

"Devil and damn, woman, what has gotten into you?" Marcus planted his hands on his lean hips, finally looking angry. "You'd think you didn't have the first inkling of how to be a lady."

She didn't—but she couldn't tell him that. The knot of frustration in her chest tightened.

"I'm doing my *best*." *For you, you ungrateful nodcock.*

"If you'd care to do better," he said in icy tones, "I'm sure

Mama would be perfectly happy to introduce you to new acquaintances and—"

"I don't want your mother's help, I want *you*, you bacon-brained lummox!" she exploded. Provoked beyond words, she paced before the gaping cabinets, in her agitation barely holding onto her polished accent. "I don't want to make acquaintances who gossip behind my back. Who say you married beneath you and wait for me to make a mistake—any mistake—so they can pounce on it and tear me to shreds over tea and sandwiches. Who all secretly agree that I stole you from Perfect Miss Pilkington, who would have made you a much better marchioness and who still casts blooming calf eyes at you—"

Strong arms caught her at the waist, cutting off her tirade. She struggled furiously, but it was of no use. He held her against his unyielding frame.

"Penny. Look at me."

Chest heaving, she glared up at him... and despite her tumult, the warmth in his steel blue eyes sent a quiver through her belly. A melting sensation that went all the way down her spine. All at once, she was acutely aware of his hard muscle surrounding her, his scent and heat.

"I don't want Miss Pilkington. I want you," he said.

Suddenly, Penny realized how she sounded—like a jealous harpy. She felt small, stupid.

"I know that," she muttered to his chest.

"The reason I've been out so much is because I wanted to give you space to settle into your new life. To make our home how you wish without tripping over your husband at every step. In leaving you to your own devices, my intention was to be considerate."

Her gaze shot up.

His smile was rueful. "By the by, you're not the only one who thinks I've got bacon for brains. My man of business has grown quite exasperated with me."

"Why?"

"Because, my love, I can't concentrate on a word he says. All I seem to think about is you."

"Truly?" she breathed.

"Truly." His gaze went from warm to positively heated. His large hands roamed possessively over her back before cupping her bottom and pulling her flush against him.

Desire poured over her like sun-warmed honey as she felt the turgid proof of his words. His erection was huge, prodding unabashedly against the softness of her belly. Her sex fluttered and dampened. In a blink, anger morphed into wanting.

She looped her arms around his neck, gave him a saucy flutter of her eyelashes. "And what exactly do you think about when you think about me, Lord Blackwood?"

"I'll show you," he said.

Blooming hell, she loved it when his voice deepened like that. Loved it even more when he snatched her into his arms as if she weighed no more than thistledown and carried her into the bedchamber, tossing her onto the bed. With one knee on the mattress, he made quick work of her robe and his own, and though she'd had over a month to get used to his bold masculinity, her breath still caught at the glorious sight of him.

Strength and raw beauty infused his every aspect. His shoulders were wide and heavy, and her gaze caught for an instant on the scar on his upper left arm. The work of a sniper's bullet. It was a reminder that Marcus was all-too human, that she might have lost him before they'd even begun, a notion that spurred her pulse.

Not wanting to linger in fear, her eyes followed the chiseled planes of his chest, which were sprinkled with wiry bronze hair that she loved to rub her cheek against. The truth was she liked to touch him everywhere: loved the rippling of his muscled back beneath her palms, the hard drag of his ridged torso against her soft curves as he made love to her. In fact, it was becoming more and more difficult to maintain a ladylike composure when they were in bed. Last week, he'd driven her into such a frenzy that, of their own accord, her legs had wrapped around his lean hips, but he hadn't seemed to mind. His eyes had glazed over, his thrusts getting harder, deeper, filling her so utterly...

Desire sang in her blood. She couldn't help but stretch up her arms, whispering, "Come to me."

He took her outstretched arms... and she blinked to find them pinned above her head, his large hand securing her by the wrists.

"In good time," he said. "Stay like that for me, love."

Goose pimples prickled over her skin at his calm command, the passionate flare in his eyes. In the past, she would have balked at being under any man's control. She'd willingly participated in the sexual act twice before Marcus; both times, she'd taken the top position, driving the seduction along and deriving no pleasure from it. Her throat constricted as her one other experience pushed into her consciousness. Her first time and no participation on her part at all. Nothing but force, pain, and degradation...

She pushed the memory aside. With Marcus, things were different. Sex was about love and trust and goodness, dazzling discoveries that seemed to patch up her soul, healing all the broken places, leaving her whole and burning with want.

Her husband bent his head, his lips brushing hers, but when she leaned upward to deepen the kiss, his mouth left to course instead along her jaw, her neck, and collarbones. Her lungs strained as he licked a trail between her heaving breasts; when his lips closed around one throbbing nipple, a moan scraped from her throat. He'd recently introduced her to this heady pleasure. Her spine arched at the hot, drugging pull of his lips, which elicited a twin pulsing between her legs.

"I love your breasts, Penny." He licked the other taut peak, blowing softly. "They're so sweet."

"Have more then," she purred.

His husky laugh warmed her nipple. "If you insist."

He continued to playfully explore, pressing kisses over her

ribcage, her belly. She squirmed, giggling when his tongue dipped into her navel. But when his mouth continued its journey downward, she stilled. Surely, he didn't mean to kiss her... *there?* Being no well-bred miss, she accounted herself well-informed when it came to the variety of sexual acts and thus had heard about oral stimulation but, to her knowledge, that was a thing done by women to men. It hadn't occurred to her that a man—never mind a gentleman like Marcus—would wish to put his mouth on a woman's...

The first, hot swipe of his tongue startled a whimper from her. The second made her back bow off the bed. "Oh, God. Oh, *Marcus*—"

He lifted his head. "All right, Penny?"

"Yes, yes," she gasped.

"So sweet. Here like everywhere else," he muttered. "God, I can't get enough of you..."

Dazed, she let her head fall back as pleasure—as *Marcus*—consumed her. He knew no shame, his big hands holding her thighs spread as his tongue delved deeply, searching out her innermost secrets. Feral sounds broke from her as he ate her sex with passionate hunger, driving her wild with his praise. How delicious he found her. How luscious and wet. Pleasure built inside her, a storm that pushed the very boundaries of her soul. He licked upwards, to the top of her cleft, latching onto her pearl and suckling hard. Stars flashed the instant before she flew apart.

Glittering pieces. Brilliant and ecstatic. Reborn.

Caught up in the rippling waves of her climax, she nonetheless felt another jolt when he came inside her. A hard, thick filling that shoved out her tattered breath and replaced it with pure joy. More rolling tides of pleasure.

His face was dark with passion above her. "Christ, you feel good. So wet and tight, so beautiful." He ground his hips, grazing her sensitive peak with the steely root of his cock. "I'd die happy right where I am."

"You feel even better," she moaned. "So big and hard. I can't get enough of you."

The moment the words slipped out, she realized her mistake. No lady would say such things. It was one thing to flirt with one's husband and quite another to express such direct and lusty feelings.

Heart pounding, she opened her mouth to somehow take it back... but Marcus' lips claimed hers with primal force. His tongue thrust into her mouth, a hot, fierce parry that mimicked the pounding of his hips. His rhythm went from demanding to savage. Lost in the maelstrom, she clung to him, her pelvis lifting to take what he gave her, deeper and deeper, and when he groaned her name, shuddering, she felt him touch the end of her, his heat flooding her womb. Then the storm broke inside her, the tumultuous bliss almost too much to bear.

Eventually, Marcus rolled onto his back, tucking her against his side. With her cheek nestled against his chest, she lay dazed, listening to his heart which thudded as furiously as her own. For long moments only the sound of their ragged breaths filled the room. Then her mind began to work again, and anxiety whirled. *Did I reveal too much? Shock him with my behavior? Does he suspect...?*

A rumbling chuckle interrupted her spiraling thoughts. Lifting her head, she saw her husband's smiling expression.

"What is so amusing?" she said.

He threaded his fingers through the hair at her temple, tucking a long strand behind her ear. His touch was intimate, loving, and God help her but her insides melted just a little bit more.

"Us," he said. "I never thought I'd want a bickering sort of marriage, but if the way we just concluded our first row is any indication, I think we should have more of them."

"We don't have to fight to make love," she pointed out.

"True. But you must admit that was rather vigorous,"—he waggled his brows—"even for us."

Biting her lip, she ventured, "It wasn't... too vigorous?"

"You can't be serious."

She didn't know how to reply in a way that wouldn't betray her true fears. In the next instant, she found herself on her back, caged by Marcus' lean strength.

His eyes searched her face. "Pandora, you truly don't know how good we are together?"

"I do. It's just that..." *I'm not who you think I am. I'm not good enough for you. I live in constant fear that you'll discover the truth and hate me...* She swallowed and settled for a part of the truth. "I don't know if other wives get as, um, carried away as I do."

"Probably not."

Her stomach plummeted at his words.

"Which is why I pity their husbands and thank God in my prayers for bringing you to my balcony that night." The tenderness in Marcus' eyes, in his hands as they cupped her face, stole her breath. "In our bed, in our lives, I want us to be honest with one another. Always. No rule but love between us. You're special, my own lucky Penny, and I want you exactly the way you are."

"I don't deserve you." Her voice hitched. *But I love you too much to ever let you go.*

"Even if I'm a bacon-brained lummox?" He grinned at her.

"You're the best of husbands, I adore you, and we'll never fight again," she declared.

He laughed outright. "Don't make promises you can't keep, love. Why don't we make a different pact? Even if we fight, we'll never go to sleep angry with each other, nor will we sleep apart. No matter how bad it is, we'll hash out our differences before we go to bed."

She loved the idea. "And once we're there—in bed, I mean—we'll make up?"

His smile turned wicked. "Thoroughly, my love. You can count on that."

8

OCTOBER 1829

Penny tore her gaze from the flames in the hearth back to the half-written letter on the escritoire in front of her. The loops of ink swam, and she blinked away tears to focus on the words she was composing to her closest friend and confidante. A woman she hadn't seen in over twelve years but who knew all her secrets, her dark corners, and who had, in truth, helped lead her into the light.

Dipping her pen into the inkwell, she continued writing. She used the old code that Flora—now known as Sister Agatha—had taught her all those years ago. To outsiders, the letter read as polite correspondence concerning a charity of which Pandora was a patron. Deciphering the code, Sister Agatha would find the following:

... I've done everything I can to please him. His favorite foods, tranquility at home, apologies... nothing is working. Despair fills me, and I wish you were here to tell me what to do, my wisest friend. How do I win back the heart of the man I love...?

A droplet fell onto the paper, splotching the ink.

Sighing, Penny completed and sealed the letter, addressing it to the humble manor in Oxfordshire where Sister Agatha, along with other godly women, carried out their good works. Once a convent, the site had lost its official title when King Henry VIII banned religious communities altogether. Yet the Society of St. Margery had continued to discreetly administer to the poor and needy under the guise of running a school; the place had been affectionately dubbed the Abbey by the locals. Now, with successive relief acts loosening the strictures on religious practice, the sisters were able to practice their faith and charity more openly.

Flora had joined the Abbey over a decade ago. After the death of Harry, she'd wanted nothing more to do with espionage, which she'd participated in purely for her husband's sake. She'd longed to dedicate the rest of her life to doing good works and had her eye on the Society of St. Margery for some time. But she'd waited until Pandora's future was settled before she made her announcement that she meant to end her old life in order to start a new one.

Pandora could still recall their last parting in Brussels. She'd gripped her friend's hands, looked into the warm brown eyes that had been a source of comfort and wisdom since she was a ten-year-old girl and couldn't help but plead for the other to change her mind.

"But you can't join a religious society! You must come to London with me, Flora. You could play the part of my mama, which you are in every way but blood. You could chaperone me, help me win Marcus' heart—"

"My darling girl, you don't need my help for that." Giving her a squeeze in return, Flora pulled free, walking to the window that overlooked the apartment's small garden. Sunshine slanted over her handsome, weathered features. "If this Lieutenant-Colonel Harrington is half the man you say he is, he will be entirely smitten with you at first glance. He'll have the good sense to snatch you off the marriage mart before any other gentleman has the chance."

Pandora flushed. "I wish I had your confidence. But I don't know how to be a lady—which I'll have to be to woo a gentleman like Marcus. You come from the *ton,* Flora. You could help me, be with me..." Her chest clutched at the thought of losing her only friend. "I need you."

"What you need, dearest, is a husband. And seeing as you've already met the man of your dreams—although he doesn't know it,"—Flora's eyes had a mischievous sparkle—"you will soon have the fulfilment that you deserve. The kind that I had with Harry."

Seeing that sparkle die, snuffed out by sorrow that two years hadn't dulled, Pandora said softly, "I miss Harry, too. Every day."

"I know, dear." Flora's hand went to the plain silver locket that hung in the starched folds of her chemisette. Pandora knew it contained a portrait of Harry as a young man, his face unlined and eyes bright with the promise of the future. "But he's gone, and I must find a way to go on. And I can't—not as Flora Hudson, who belongs too entirely to her Harry."

"Flora," Pandora whispered.

Steady brown eyes held hers. "Now that I know you will be settled, I can let Flora go. She will accompany her husband with a free heart, knowing that their daughter has found the love she so greatly deserves. And when the world believes that Flora Hudson is gone, I will be free to start over. To pursue a new life, one of peace and contemplation, one where I can administer to those in need."

I need you, she thought but didn't say because she loved Flora too much to want anything but happiness for the other. Managing to keep most of the quiver out of her voice, Pandora said, "I'm going to miss you."

Flora's arms circled her in a hug. "As I shall miss you, my dearest girl."

As the years passed, they'd kept in touch by letter, though by necessity their communications had to be guarded and infrequent. To the world, Flora Hudson was dead. Only Pandora knew that Flora's bright flame still lived on within Sister Agatha, the Abbey's guiding light.

She tried to imagine what her friend would recommend for her present situation. Knowing Agatha, the advice would likely involve being honest, repenting for one's sins, maybe even groveling... but Penny had done plenty of all three in the past fortnight, and her husband hadn't softened one iota toward her. Sighing, she set about completing her evening ablutions when she heard footsteps in the hallway outside. The familiar, precise cadence spurred her heartbeat.

Marcus. He'd come home.

Since his decree that she would give him time to decide their futures, she'd not been alone with him. They were together during the time spent with the children, but after the boys went off to their lessons, Marcus left too. He returned to sup with the family and left again after the boys retired to bed. She guessed that he was spending time at his club—at least, that was where she hoped he was going. Her insides knotted at the possibility of Marcus indulging in any other sort of nightly pleasures.

He's a good man. A loyal one. He'd never break his vows.

At the same time, she knew what a hot-blooded man he was, and he hadn't been to her bed for over a month. During the entire length of their marriage that had never happened before. Even when she had her monthly flux, he slept with her, cuddling and tucking her in close. And the fact that they couldn't make love in the usual fashion during those times didn't stop them from pleasuring one another. Her nipples tingled beneath her flannel robe as she recalled the last time she'd awakened Marcus with a kiss, his sleepy growl as she'd taken his morning cockstand deep into her mouth...

God, she missed him. And he was just next door.

True, he'd told her to stay away, to give him space until such time as he was ready... but it'd been two weeks already, and he showed no signs of thawing toward her. Perhaps he needed a nudge, a reminder of the love they shared? If this frosty state of affairs between them was allowed to continue, he might freeze her out completely... and then where would she be?

No, she thought, chewing on her lip, she had to nip things in the bud before they worsened. But how? What was the best approach to take with a husband who was furious and had every right to be?

What she needed was... an excuse. A reason to go to him that wouldn't seem like a willful infringement of the boundaries he'd set between them. Something that wouldn't anger him further. Standing before her vanity, she flipped through the possibilities. He'd wanted her to carry on with her roles as mother and marchioness... so some household problem she needed assistance with then. She drummed her fingers against the vanity's smooth surface, her perfume bottles rattling in their silver tray. A domestic quandary that her poor little female brain couldn't handle without his help...

The annual winter ball. Perfect.

Why the blooming hell didn't I think of this earlier?

Hurriedly, she checked her appearance in the looking glass. Her hair was still drying from her bath, tumbling in loose waves down her back—just the way Marcus liked it. Knowing his preference for natural beauty, she pinched her cheeks to add color rather than applying paint. Her eyes were already bright with nervous anticipation, so there was no need to do anything there. She spent another ten minutes going through her wardrobe before changing into a peignoir and slip made of ivory satin. Although demure in color, the matching set had a sophisticated cut and was edged with sensual lace, providing a dramatic foil to her dark coloring.

She paused at the door between their adjoining bedchambers. Given the state of their relationship, it seemed too bold to enter that way, and if he'd locked that private door against her, she didn't want to discover that painful knowledge. Blowing out a breath, she headed out toward the proper entrance to Marcus' room.

She found his door slightly ajar. She rapped quietly, and when there was no response, she exhaled, pushed through, and entered. The chamber was empty.

"Marcus?" she called.

No reply. Had he come home—only to go out again? Had she missed him because she'd taken too long choosing her blasted outfit?

Swallowing her disappointment, she couldn't bring herself to leave. Not just yet. The familiarity of his bedchamber wrapped around her like a blanket. She loved this room because she'd spent considerable effort decorating it, searching for and finding the exact right pieces to create a refuge both masculine and comfortable for her husband. She'd chosen a subtle pale grey-on-grey damask for the walls, a rich navy Aubusson rug to grace the floor. The handsome mahogany furnishings suited Marcus' preference for clean, classical lines.

She trailed her fingertips down a poster of the heavy tester bed and over the crisp linen sheets. She leaned over to smell his pillow, the scent of musk and sandalwood pressing on her bruised heart... and that was when she heard the noise. A faint splash.

From the bathing room.

You should go. Leave him to his privacy.

Her feet showed no intention of following her head's advice, instead taking her toward the dressing room. She passed orderly rows of jackets and waistcoats, shelves of shirts and cravats that Gibson, Marcus' valet, kept in meticulous order. She neared the door of the bathing chamber, which was partially closed, wisps of citrus-scented steam drifting out. The gentle lap of water drew her closer. She peered through the crack.

Marcus.

Blooming hell, he was gorgeous.

He was lying in the large copper tub at the center of the room, which was tiled in black and white. A fire crackled in the hearth behind him. From her vantage point, she could see his side profile, his dark, wet hair pushed back from his chiseled face. His eyes were closed, his head resting against the back lip of the tub, one sinewy arm draped along its edge. His splayed knees were visible, and the muscles of his other arm were bunching, flexing as...

Oh my goodness.

Her heart shot into her throat. At the same time, molten heat flooded her sex, her nipples prickling against her satin negligee. Because she'd caught her proper husband in the act of doing something unexpected.

Unexpectedly naughty, that was.

Was he thinking of her... or someone else? At the latter thought, fire leapt inside her, possessiveness feeding into her arousal. Because Marcus was *hers*—and if he didn't know that, then she would have to prove it to him.

9

"**R**ide me, love," he growled.

With his back against the headboard and his hands clamped on his wife's sweet arse, he urged her on—not that she needed much encouragement. Goddamn, he'd married a hot little vixen. She wriggled her hips, grounding down, and the feel of her tight sheath taking his cock to the root nearly drew his fire. But he held on, wanting to prolong the pleasure, the joy of introducing his beloved to her first good fucking.

For the first three months of their marriage, he'd made gentle love to his new bride, not wanting to scare her or offend her delicate sensibilities. He'd planned to introduce her slowly to the more adventurous delights of the marital bed. But his marchioness turned out to be an eager pupil, and each time he bedded her, the passion between them flared ever hotter. Tonight he'd judged her ready to try a new position... one that would become as necessary as it was pleasurable as the months went on.

One of his hands moved forward to rest possessively on the slight swell of her belly. She was hardly showing, yet the idea of her ripening with his child filled him with a potent combination of tenderness and lust. He didn't know why, but the sight of his pregnant wife made him randier than hell.

As luck would have it, being with child seemed to affect Penny in the same way.

"Marcus." His name had never sounded better than at this moment, her voice breathless as she bounced on his erection, her hair a wild and glorious tangle over her shoulders. "Oh, I'm so close…"

Hell, he should have had her astride him weeks ago.

"Lean over, there's a love." He slid his palms up her smooth shoulder blades, pulling her closer to his chest. "Take me like this."

He saw and felt the moment that the new angle hit her: flames leapt in her gorgeous eyes, her cheeks flushing as she sank down on his shaft, her lips forming a soundless O as her pussy gripped his rod like a velvet fist. Lungs straining, he guided her hips, grinding her against him, rubbing her little love knot against his cock with each plunging stroke.

"Marcus… I can't… it's too… *oh my God.*"

She came, her sex milking him, bringing him to the edge.

Marcus' eyes snapped open.

He became aware of several things at once. His lungs were pulling harshly, his burgeoned cock throbbing in the wet fist of his own hand. He was a hairsbreadth from shooting his seed… but something had jolted him from his fantasy.

A sound, a furtive movement.

He hastily released himself, water sloshing as he sat up. He'd told Gibson, his valet, to give him privacy. The man had been with him through the wars and usually followed orders as well as any soldier.

"That you, Gibson?" he called out. "I'm not finished yet. Come back in a half hour."

No reply. Had he imagined the noise?

After another minute, Marcus relaxed and sank back into the hot, sudsy water. Absently, he stroked his still rigid shaft... but the mood had been broken. Anger now simmered along with arousal, a frustrating and potent mix.

Why in the devil was he fantasizing about Pandora? After her betrayal—the lies that had destroyed everything he held dear—he should want nothing to do with her. She'd manipulated him for the entire length of their marriage, and he probably didn't even know the full extent of it. Hell, he didn't *want* to know. What man wanted to discover just how much of a lovesick dupe he'd been?

At the same time, he couldn't shake the image of her on her knees, begging for his forgiveness. What she'd shared of her past made his chest clench. If she could be believed—the operative word being *if*—then the suffering she'd known... He rubbed his hands over his steam-slicked face, swamped by a feeling of protectiveness that he couldn't control.

He wanted to kill that bastard Octavian for coercing Penny, a bleeding ten-year-old *orphan* for Christ's sake, into the dirty business of espionage. She might not have called it coercion, but to Marcus it was. She'd had no other choice—besides stealing or starving, that was, and he didn't count those as real choices. Octavian had taken advantage of her, trained her to do his filthy bidding. Marcus wanted to tear out the man's bloody throat for treating his Penny that way.

Back then, I thought of it as completing a mission. Her words were a haunting echo in his head. *It was the only life I knew. I didn't think I deserved any better.*

His fury reared again, along with a pain that sliced through him as excruciatingly as a surgeon's scalpel. And he would know as he'd once had a bullet removed from his shoulder. The only thing that had made the agony bearable had been the alternative: had the assassin shot him three inches over, he'd have been dead on the spot.

Even so, he'd take a dozen bullets over knowing that Pandora had been with other men. That she'd not thought herself worthy of a better life. That she'd bartered her beautiful body as if it were naught but a cheap commodity.

Jealousy and rage scalded his insides. For so long, he'd thought of her as exclusively his. His virgin bride, his precious wife, his one and only love. To accept that she'd lain with others and that she'd *lied* to him about it...

Everything I did was because I loved you so much and knew that you'd never love me back as Pandora Smith.

Bloody hell, *would* he have married her had he known the truth of her origins and all that she'd done? His gut knotted; he didn't know the answer. Yet the thought of never having been wed to her, never knowing the love and laughter and passion they'd shared, never having the boys...

His eyes shut, his head falling back against the tub. It was too bloody much to contend with. Pressure roiled in his head, his groin. God, he just needed to release some of his pent-up frustration...

He fisted himself again. He tried to summon up a fantasy that didn't involve Penny... but it was impossible. From the moment they'd met, she'd been his every desire. His one and only. Cursing himself a fool, he couldn't deny that the past month hadn't changed that fact for him one whit. He still lusted after his damned wife. A woman who'd made a fool of him. He frigged himself harder, the water slapping against the tub. Her name wrenched from him in a tortured groan as his pleasure spiked, his balls tautening.

"Marcus?"

His eyes snapped open; his gaze locked with Penny's through the haze of steam. Heart pounding, his blood rushing hot in his veins, for one disorienting moment, he didn't know whether this was part of his fantasy or reality. The distinction didn't become any clearer when she shrugged off her robe, revealing a sensual slip of creamy satin and lace. She untied the bow on her left shoulder, his mouth watering as the bodice fell, revealing one perfect round breast crowned with a ripe cherry nipple. She untied the bow on her other shoulder, and the negligee fell completely to join her robe on the floor.

"I miss you so much," she whispered.

Hell. Bloody fucking hell.

His vision darkened, and the next instant, he was out of the tub. He didn't have time to think, didn't want to. His primal instinct took over, and he reached for what was his.

Relief. Desire. Excitement.

The emotions hit her simultaneously, a barrage that left her breathless.

Her pulse leapt as Marcus stalked toward her, water sluicing off his lean, hard form—and by all that was holy, he was hard *everywhere*. Her gaze dipped to his groin, and her knees quivered. His cock was huge and thick, boldly erect, his bollocks swinging heavily between his muscled thighs as he prowled towards her. Jerking her gaze back up, she saw his eyes were smoldering and heavy-lidded.

All man, her husband.

Everything she'd ever wanted.

He reached for her at the same time that she reached for him. Their bodies collided, the impact of hard and soft sending a shock of pleasure through her system. His kiss was crushing, equal parts hunger and anger, and she didn't care. Having him back was more than she deserved. More than she'd hoped for when she made her daring play a moment ago. Moaning, she reached up, winding her arms around his neck, closing the distance between them in the only way she knew how.

An instant later, she was driven backward, her back meeting with hard smooth tile. Her neck arched against the wall as his lips closed around her nipple—not gently as he'd done in the past but with a ferocity that made her gasp aloud. The edge of his teeth grazed her, and her pussy clenched. When he suckled hard, wetness gushed between her legs.

Then his mouth was back on hers, claiming and savage, and the glory of it made her wild. Her fingers tangling in his wet hair, she rubbed herself shamelessly against him, whimpering as her budded nipples dragged against the taut planes of his chest, the wiry hair an exquisite friction. Lower, she felt his poker-hard staff prodding her belly, so she pressed even closer, wanting it, wanting *him* with every fiber of who she was.

All of a sudden, she was lifted off the ground, her back against the wall, Marcus between her spread legs. His eyes glittering, he notched his cock to her and brought her down on the rearing shaft. All the way. So deep his head nudged her womb. No sooner had the pleasured whimper left her then he did it again, lifting her and slamming her down on his rod.

On the third rise and fall, she flew apart. Her entire being convulsed around the thickness holding her aloft, piercing her very core, the heart of who she was. Through the misty bliss, she heard him grunt, the slapping of flesh as he drove into her again and again. She held onto him, her hands clutching his bunching biceps, her legs circling his flexing hips, so she felt and heard his fulfillment. His powerful body quaked against her, his groan reverberating against the tiles.

Dazed, happy, she inhaled the scent of him, stroked the slick muscles of his back. It was heaven to be with him this way again. Words tumbled through her head.

I love you. I've missed you. Forgive me, and I swear I won't lie to you again.

She searched for the right thing to say.

He pulled out so abruptly that she gasped. Her feet landed on the slippery tiles, and the moment she gained her balance, he let her go. Leaning over, he retrieved her clothes from the ground.

"Get dressed." He tossed the items at her.

She caught them out of reflex, clutching the satin to her chest. Happiness evaporated the instant she saw Marcus' face. Hard jaw, harder eyes. He turned from her, and wrapping a towel around his waist, headed for the doorway.

Stunned, she said, "Where are you going?"

"Out," he said curtly.

"But after we... I mean, we just..." she stammered, "we ought to talk..."

"We fucked, Pandora." His harsh words cut short her breath. "If you think to manipulate me with your sexual charms, think again. Your wiles no longer work on me. I will take as much time as I want to decide upon our future, and you have no say about it. Now I'm going out. When I return, I'll expect you back in your own room."

Silent, her lungs straining for air, she tried to summon a reply.

Brushing past her as if she were invisible, he stalked out.

10

1819

"Milady, it isn't safe for you—"

"I'll be quite alright." Penny cut the footman off in tones that brooked no argument. "Wait here at the carriage. I shall return shortly."

She headed down the narrow lane framed on both sides by leaning, ramshackle tenements. The air was choked with smoke from cooking fires, and lines of wash crisscrossed overhead, the garments swaying like limp flags of surrender. Poverty was an invincible enemy, but to Penny's mind, the inhabitants of this small street on the fringes of St. Giles were still fighting the good fight. At least the folk here still bothered to cook and do laundry —which was more than she could say for some of the places she'd lived growing up.

Poor but not yet beaten, she thought, tucking away the information.

As an agent, she'd learned that information was power. A spy was only as good as her informants and the knowledge they passed her way. In the nearly two years that Penny had lived amongst the *ton*, she'd come to understand that the Upper Crust operated by similar principles and thus her visit today. She found the address she was looking for and, gathering up her pale blue skirts, climbed up the creaky steps.

Arriving at her destination, she rapped her kidskin-covered knuckles against the peeling wood. She heard shuffling from inside, a high-pitched voice quickly shushed. The flat had no windows, not even a peephole on the door.

A voice emerged from the other side of the barrier. "Who is it?"

"The Marchioness of Blackwood," Penny said.

Silence. The door cracked open. A thin, ginger-haired woman in her twenties peered out, her light brown eyes widening beneath her cap at the sight of Penny.

"Milady," she stammered and bobbed an uncertain curtsy.

"Miss Randall," Penny said pleasantly. "I have a proposition to discuss. I'd rather do it indoors, if I may?"

Blinking, the woman stepped aside, and Penny entered, taking in her surroundings at a glance. Seeing as the place consisted of a single cramped room, there wasn't much to see, and, in truth, the space was much like Miss Randall: destitute and tidy. What drew Penny's attention was the small table at the center of the room.

Sitting there upon a rickety chair was a young red-haired girl —four or five, by Penny's guess—working stitches into a piece of cloth. She was a pretty little moppet, her hair tamed into two pristine and elegant braids. She was dressed similarly to her mama in a plain, worn frock that was meticulously patched, pressed, and free of stains. The work of someone who had perfected their craft and would practice it regardless of circumstance.

"Who are you?" the girl said, her eyes rounding.

"Molly, mind your manners." Miss Randall went over to her child, her stance protective. "This is 'er ladyship, the Marchioness of Blackwood. Do your curtsy now."

The girl scrambled to her feet and followed her mama's instruction.

"Very pretty, Miss Molly," Penny said, smiling.

"Thank you, milady." The child's dimples peeped out.

"Molly, you may see if Mary is free to play," her mama said. "'Alf hour only, mind you. Then back to sewing."

Molly's eyes lit up, and she skipped out the door. The instant the girl was gone, her mother said curtly, "How may I help you, milady?"

Yes, everything Penny observed today matched with what she'd learned about Jenny Randall and strengthened her confidence in her plan.

"I've come to hire you," she said.

Miss Randall's lips trembled. "Is this some sort o' jest?"

Penny could see why the other might think so. After all, Jenny Randall had been publicly dismissed and humiliated last week by her former employer, Lady Auberville, one of the *ton*'s reigning hostesses. Being a nasty sort, Lady Auberville had fired Miss Randall in front of her entire staff. Then she'd spewed vitriol concerning her maid's sordid secret far and wide in Society. Everyone who was anyone now knew that Jenny Randall, a once respectable and sought-after ladies maid, had borne a child out of wedlock. Her prospects for a good position were forever ruined by her ex-mistress' malicious tongue and love of hysterics.

Imagine, the wages I've paid the ungrateful trollop have been going toward her bastard's upkeep, Lady Auberville had shrilled to all and sundry. *I dismissed her right away, of course; I had to set an example. One cannot allow such immortality to taint one's household.*

Which was the height of hypocrisy, considering Lord Auberville had at least three by-blows with the mistress he kept. But that was the *ton* for you, Penny thought in disgust.

"I'm not jesting," she said steadily. "I am in need of a ladies maid, and you happen to be the best. As you also happen to be out of a position at present, I think we're an excellent match."

Miss Randall stared at her. "You know... 'bout Molly. She hasn't got a father."

"More credit to you for taking such fine care of her," Penny said. "Which brings me to the details of my offer. I'll pay you double the wages you received from Lady Auberville, along with a bonus to start, so that you may find Molly suitable lodgings close to work. We'll arrange your schedule so that you may see her every day, and you'll have holidays too—all paid, of course."

Hope flared in Miss Randall's eyes, snuffed quickly by disbelief. She said in a taut voice, "I don't understand, milady. You—you could 'ave any maid. Why would you be wanting... someone like me?"

Because you made a mistake and did the best you could under the circumstances. You deserve a helping hand—and not to be judged by all the blooming Lady Aubervilles of the world.

Aloud, Penny said briskly, "As I've explained, I want the best. I've seen your work: with Lady Osterly, Mrs. Jones-Sykes, and then with Lady Auberville. You transformed three dowdy matrons into ladies of the utmost style."

Miss Randall bit her lip and remained silent. The fact that she didn't comment upon her former employers' lack of fashion sense —or their sense in general—raised her even higher in Penny's estimation. By Penny's accounting, Jenny Randall was well within her rights to flay her last vicious mistress to pieces... but she didn't. She took the high road instead. This spoke volumes about her judgement, loyalty, and discretion—qualities worth their weight in gold.

"The job of being my ladies maid won't be easy," Penny went on. "I'll expect you to keep abreast of the latest fashions and trends. Modistes, milliners, hairdressers—it will be your responsibility to find me the very best. I won't settle for less."

"Of course. But your ladyship... you're already lovely."

"My aim is to be more than lovely. I want to make my husband and my son proud," Penny said with frank determination. "I mean to elevate the Blackwood name to the highest echelons, and I am not yet there."

Since the birth of James, she'd worked hard to improve her social standing. Her circle of acquaintances now rivaled Cora Pilkington's, and her parties were well attended. She wasn't yet the marchioness that Marcus deserved, but, with the right help, she would get there. From what she'd seen of Jenny Randall's work and manner, the maid would be a valuable addition to her team.

"I reckon I would make a few changes 'ere and there," Miss Randall ventured shyly. "If you don't mind my saying, with your coloring and looks, I'd dress you in bolder colors and styles, milady, so as to stand out. Sometimes, it's not so much about following a craze, but *starting* one... if you get my meaning."

"See? I knew you were the one I was looking for," Penny said.

Miss Randall's cheeks turned pink.

"But I haven't yet finished discussing my requirements. In addition to fashion and the like, I will expect you to report any gossip you hear to me. You and I both know that the servants' talk travels faster than any other. They're the first to know the best and worst of everything that goes on in the *ton*—and I want to know too." Penny paused. "I will also expect that, when it comes to what goes on in my household, you'll keep a discreet tongue."

"Yes, milady." Miss Randall nodded. "I han't e'er spoken ill of my employers."

"You'll find I'm a fair employer who rewards loyalty, talent, and hard work." Penny held out her hand. "Now have we come to an agreement, Miss Randall?"

The maid's eyes shimmered, and her hand suddenly shot out, gripping Penny's.

"God bless you," she said, her voice hitching.

With prickling embarrassment, Penny said, "There's no need

for that. Just know that if you do me a good turn, Miss Randall, I shall return the favor."

"It's Jenny, milady." A smile transformed the maid's thin face, and she bobbed a curtsy. "You 'ave my word that I'll do a good job. I swear,"—her words were earnest, her face turning serious—"I won't let you down."

11

NOVEMBER 1829

"I think we should hang poison ivy instead of holly for your Winter Ball."

"Good idea," Penny said absently.

"See? I *told* you she wasn't listening."

Silence followed, and Penny hastily returned her attention to the four female visitors in her drawing room. Wary by nature and from experience, she had numerous acquaintances but few close friends. The recent trouble with the Spectre, however, had brought her into contact with the Kents.

The family was unconventional to say the least. Coming from middling class origins in the countryside, the intrepid Kent siblings had managed—apparently without design—to take Society by storm. The eldest brother, Ambrose Kent, had once been a Thames River Policeman. Somehow he'd ended up marrying the former Lady Marianne Draven, one of the *ton's* richest and most glamorous widows. After his marriage, he'd started a private enquiry business, and Kent & Associates had quickly grown to become one of London's most respected investigative firms.

Several months back, when the Spectre had risen to blackmail Penny, she'd turned to Kent and his partners out of desperation. Back then, she'd have done anything to keep Marcus from knowing her past. Not only had Kent proved of assistance, but his wife and sisters had wholeheartedly taken on Penny's cause as well. Apparently, the ladies often got involved in Kent's cases (to his dismay and that of their husbands), and not only had the women helped Penny, they'd brought her into their fold.

To Penny's surprise, she had let them.

At present, each of her friends wore an expression unique to their personalities. Kent's wife, Marianne, a stunning silver blonde around Penny's age, regarded her with knowing and compassionate emerald eyes. Emma, the eldest Kent sister, was a pretty brunette with an earnest air. Over a year ago, she'd landed the catch of the *ton*, the Duke of Strathaven, a once notorious rake; now the duchess had a slight furrow between her brows as if she were trying to decipher Penny's state of mind. Sitting next to her, Dorothea, Emma's sister and the newlywed Marchioness of Tremont, regarded Penny with concern in her gentle hazel gaze.

Lastly, Miss Violet Kent, the youngest of the bunch and the one who'd been speaking, had triumph written over her vivid features. Probably because she'd made her point: Penny *hadn't* been listening. She'd been caught up yet again in her tumultuous thoughts about Marcus and the state of her marriage.

"Hush, Violet," Emma said. "This isn't the time or place."

"But you know I'm right. Lady Pandora doesn't seem herself at all—"

"Why don't you go check on the boys, dear?" Thea's tone was kind yet firm. "Make sure Fredward isn't terrorizing the Blackwood boys?"

Fredward referred to Frederick and Edward, Thea's stepson and Marianne's son, respectively. The nine-year-olds were so

inseparable that the Kent family had given them a shared nick-
name, and they'd become favorite playmates of Penny's boys.

Collecting herself, Penny said wryly, "I doubt anyone could
terrorize my sons. If anything, probably the opposite is true."

"Well, let's minimize the bloodshed at any rate. Do run along,
Violet," Marianne said.

Violet rose nimbly to her feet, rolling her tawny eyes as she
did so. "No one ever listens to me," she grumbled in a way that
suggested this might be a refrain. "And I don't know why I have to
leave just when the conversation is getting good."

After her lithe figure disappeared through the doorway, Thea
said, "I do apologize for my sister, Pandora. Vi's just used to
speaking her mind."

"Her honesty is refreshing," Penny assured her.

"I agree—but unfortunately the *ton* doesn't," the duchess said
with a sigh. "If Violet doesn't learn to curb her tongue and manner
at least a *little*, she's going to land in hot water. And after her
behavior at the Waterson's affair last week, the scandal broth is
already at a simmer."

Penny had been so preoccupied by her own state of affairs that
she'd missed the gossip. "What happened?" she asked.

"Nothing really. Violet was just being Violet," Thea said.

From what she knew of the high-spirited Miss Kent, that
could mean most anything.

"I *told* her not to dance more than twice with any gentleman.
But the moment my back was turned, she was off like a shot. And
it was a waltz, too," Emma huffed.

"I suppose we can't blame her. Mr. Murray is one of the most
sought after bucks in Town," Marianne said, "if rather too aware
of that fact."

"Wickham Murray?" Penny sat up straighter.

"Yes." Thea's honey-brown locks tipped to one side. "Do you
know him?"

"He's the younger brother of Viscount Carlisle, one of Blackwood's cronies." At the thought of her husband, her heart throbbed.

"I don't think I've met this Carlisle," Emma said.

"He's not much for Society. Prefers his estate in Scotland or his lodge in the country." She couldn't help but wrinkle her nose. "He's always struck me as a bit high in the instep, a rigid, traditional sort of man. Quite the opposite in temperament and looks of his charming younger brother. But Blackwood swears Carlisle's a good chap and a gentleman's gentleman, whatever that means."

"That doesn't sound too promising." Thea nibbled on her lower lip. "Violet doesn't do well with rigidity or tradition. If she's truly forming an attachment to Wickham and his older brother doesn't approve—"

"We'll cross that bridge when we get there," Marianne said firmly. "No matter what happens, we'll support Vi in finding the happiness she deserves."

As the other two murmured their agreement, Penny felt her throat thicken. From the start, she'd admired the close bonds between the Kents. Although like any family they had their share of squabbles and disagreements, they also seemed to greet each other's quirks and foibles with unwavering acceptance. It was the sort of love that Pandora hadn't encountered until she'd met Flora and Harry... that she'd believed she had with Marcus.

The despair that she'd been holding back surged to the fore. Since the episode in the bathing room ten days ago, nothing had changed between her and Marcus. No, not nothing: things had gotten *worse*. Now he was actively avoiding her, spending as little time as possible at home, and she had to battle growing hopelessness. Would they ever get past their impasse?

Had her lies destroyed everything?

"Well, enough about Violet. Let's get to the crux of why we're really here."

The duchess' crisp tones broke Penny's anguished reverie. She looked up, and the compassion on her friends' faces was almost more than she could bear.

"Pandora, dearest, how are things?" Thea said softly.

Don't be a blasted watering pot. Pull it together.

"Well, there's more to do, of course," she said with false cheer. "Fortunately, there are three weeks left to prepare. I'm thinking of hiring the most splendid orchestra—"

"We don't mean the ball. We mean between you and Blackwood." Although Marianne's words were blunt, her green eyes held empathy.

Given the three's involvement in her case, they knew about the Spectre and his final act of destruction: the letter that had revealed her secrets, smashing her world to smithereens. And even if they hadn't known about her clandestine past, they couldn't have missed the rumors buzzing through the *ton*. Everyone was talking about the Blackwood Estrangement.

Before the disaster had happened, Society had labelled them a love match. Marcus had accompanied her most everywhere; at balls, he'd even danced with her—something husbands rarely did with their own wives. Yet in the past week and a half, she'd showed up on her own at a few functions, which she'd attended to keep up appearances. Her solo status had started the tittering behind fans. What fueled the gossip further was that when Marcus did show, he'd paid perfunctory attention to her. He'd greeted her coolly and then went off to socialize with others.

It was bad enough that those others had included women. Being a war hero and a devastatingly virile man, Marcus had always attracted female attention. In the past, his behavior as an obviously devoted husband had discouraged interested ladies from trying to pursue an affair. Now, however, the high-kick harlots sensed blood in the water, and they'd wasted no time in circling him with hunger in their eyes.

The most persistent amongst them was the Countess of Ashley, the former Miss Cora Pilkington. The milk-fed trollop was more devious than the rest. Whilst Marcus was too upstanding a gentleman to flirt with other ladies even now— thank God—Lady Cora hid her salacious intentions behind a demure and winsome manner. Everyone knew her marriage to Ashley was an unhappy one, and she wasted no time in garnering Marcus' sympathy. Her damsel-in-distress act set Penny's teeth on edge.

On two recent occasions, Penny had seen the other clinging to Marcus' every word, wearing a doleful, worshipping expression, and she'd wanted to scratch the bitch's eyes out.

But that was neither here nor there.

"Things haven't improved between Blackwood and me." The admission made her voice rusty. "I don't know that they ever will. I've been trying... but Blackwood hasn't thawed. I don't think he can ever forgive me."

"You mustn't give up hope." Thea reached out and squeezed Penny's hand. "Your husband loves you. I'm sure he just needs time to adjust."

Leave it to Thea to think the best of every situation.

"Do you think it would help if Tremont spoke with your husband?" Thea went on. "Because he would be happy to—"

"It won't help. Blackwood doesn't want to hear about my past —least of all from my former colleague." Penny forced a smile. "And while I sincerely doubt that Tremont would be *happy* to play any part in my imbroglio, I have no doubt that he would do so at your behest, my dear."

Thea blushed. She said nothing, but then she didn't have to. It was clear to all and sundry that Tremont adored his new bride, would take the stars down from the sky if she asked. Having been acquainted with the cold and ruthless spy that Tremont had once been, Penny thought the change in her old comrade nothing short of a miracle. Then again, a sweet and innocent lady like Thea deserved no less.

"So what is your plan?"

Penny looked to Marianne. "Plan?"

"For winning Blackwood back," the blond beauty clarified.

"What I've been doing, I suppose." She shrugged to hide her frustration. "Having his favorite foods prepared, making our home an oasis of domestic tranquility. Doing my part as the perfect marchioness, which includes planning the Winter Ball to end all Winter Balls." She paused, adding wryly, "And then there's the groveling."

"Food is an excellent idea," the duchess put in. "Whenever His Grace and I have a disagreement, I find Scotch pie an excellent way to make peace."

"She makes Scotch pie at least once a week," Thea said, her hazel eyes sparkling.

"Twice," Emma said.

"Food and being the consummate hostess are all well and good," Marianne said, "but in my opinion there ought to be a limit to the groveling."

"Obviously I haven't reached it yet." Penny allowed herself a sigh. "Blackwood shows no signs of forgiving me."

"Perhaps it isn't his forgiveness you most need."

"I beg your pardon?"

Marianne smoothed the skirts of her fawn silk carriage dress. Having learned to read others as a necessary part of survival, Penny interpreted the other's gesture as preparation for saying something difficult. Marianne's next words proved her intuition right.

"I've done things that I've regretted—that many consider beyond the pale," the blonde said steadily. "One could say that, in some ways, I've been where you are now. Given the wrong that I'd done, I didn't believe I could win over a man as good and honorable as my husband."

She didn't need to say more. It was a well-known fact amongst the *ton* that her daughter, Primrose, had been born out of wedlock, the product of a youthful indiscretion. When Ambrose

Kent had wed Marianne, he'd also adopted Primrose, and the Kent family had taken the girl under their collective wing, making it clear that she was one of their own.

"How did you? Win him over, I mean?" Penny said.

"By forgiving myself. In truth, Ambrose helped me to realize that we all make mistakes, and, most importantly,"—Marianne's eyes held hers—"true love forgives."

The words struck tinder, a painful flare within Penny's chest. It took her a moment to recognize what she was feeling. The emotion was so at odds with her guilt and remorse that she hadn't paid it any mind. But the smoldering ember was there, had *been* there for days if she was honest, and it was one of... resentment.

True, she'd wronged Marcus and broken his trust. She deserved his anger... and yet didn't she also deserve at least a *chance* to make amends? He'd vowed that they would never go to bed angry with one another, yet for six weeks now, she'd endured his wrath and, worse yet, sleepless nights in a cold and lonely bed. He wouldn't listen to her, shut her out completely, and when she'd made that desperate attempt to connect with him, he'd dismissed her... like a whore.

Because that's what you are. And he doesn't even know the ugliest part of it. Imagine how he'd despise you if he knew the full truth...

Her hands balled in her lap, a vise of shame digging into her heart. She couldn't share these dark thoughts with friends—or with anyone, except for Flora. So, with skill borne out of practice, she pushed them into a mental box and locked them away until such time as she knew what to do with them. Which might prove to be never.

For the time being, she had to soldier on. Focus on her plan. Showing Marcus that she was truly contrite and that she could be a wife worthy of him were her only hopes of winning him back.

"I appreciate your concern." Her gaze included all of her guests. "Truly, I am grateful for your visit, but I think it best to persevere with my plan. I'll continue trying to please my husband,

and that includes putting on the biggest crush the *ton* has ever seen."

Steeling herself against astute glances, Penny held her smile in place.

After a moment, Marianne said quietly, "Then you must let us know how we may assist with the ball preparations."

Relief trickled through her that her friends wouldn't push her on the issue.

"I haven't even made the guest list yet," she admitted.

"If you have a pen and parchment handy, I could jot down a list," Emma volunteered. "Between all of us, we ought to know who's in Town."

"We could make a list of anything else you need too," Thea added.

Penny could think of a few things.

My husband's forgiveness.

His love.

The marriage I once had.

"Thank you. That sounds lovely," she said and smiled to hide her aching heart.

12

As the carriage rolled to a stop in front of their townhouse, Marcus' youngest son, indigo eyes wide and tone wheedling said, "Please Papa, can't we go for a walk in the square before supper?"

"We're already dressed for the snow, and it's the warmest it has been all week." His middle child took up the cause. "What would ten minutes hurt?"

Not to be bested, his eldest quoted, *"Walking is man's best medicine."*

When the rascals joined forces, they were a force to be reckoned with.

Stifling a smile, Marcus said, "Who am I to argue with Hippocrates? As long as your mama agrees."

The last words emerged from him automatically, without conscious consideration. It was a habit borne from over a decade of parenting three high-spirited boys with his wife. As it was too late to take the words back, he raised a brow at her.

Sitting on the opposite bench with their youngest, Pandora stared at him, her sooty lashes fluttering. Uncertainty flitted through her eyes, making his gut twist... with shame.

Of late, he'd been a bastard to her, and he knew it. He just didn't know how to stop. How to stem the jealous rage that roared over him at the thought of her betrayal... of her being with other men. Even now, his muscles bunched instinctively, and he had to barricade his fury.

She looked to their children, saying firmly, "No more than ten minutes." She adjusted the collar of Owen's coat and pulled his knitted cap down tightly over his dark curls. "Be sure to keep your scarves and gloves on and watch for the icy patches."

"Yes, Mama," the boys chorused.

The groom let down the steps, and the three scamps bounded out, heading for the square, their navy woolen coats and red scarves bright splashes against the snow-dusted terrain. Marcus alighted next and helped his wife down. Her boots touched lightly to the ground, her ermine-lined cloak of ruby velvet swirling gracefully around her. Wordlessly, he offered her his arm. Her eyes wide, her breath puffing in the chilled air, she took it, holding onto him tightly as they followed their children through the gates.

It was nearing dusk, and the park was empty. The setting sun cast glinting jewels over the snow-crusted ground and trees. Ice crunched beneath their feet as they trailed their sons, who were whooping and pelting each other with snowballs.

"They're little savages," Marcus remarked.

"They've just been cooped up as of late. What with the snow and the cold weather, they haven't had a chance to expend their energy," Penny said. "They're just boys being boys."

Which she would say even if the rascals committed bloody murder. Marcus felt his lips twitch. His wife always defended their offspring—even when they didn't deserve it—a tendency that he found both exasperating and adorable. And, damn it, it was good to have a normal conversation with her again. To be walking arm and arm with her, talking about their children.

Not wanting to lose the feeling, he said, "Have you forgotten that we just took them to the spectacle at Astley's? After an afternoon of watching Madame Monique le Magnifique balancing on a tightrope, I should think they've had their fair share of excitement for the day."

"Well, watching someone on a tightrope isn't the same as walking it yourself," she replied softly.

The subtext didn't escape him, and her uncharacteristic tentativeness again knotted his insides, made him want to apologize for acting like a damned cad these past two weeks. At the same time, his vulnerability when it came to his wife angered him. Having full knowledge of her deceptive nature, he would no longer countenance being played like a puppet, and yet he couldn't free himself from her strings. As the episode in his bathing room had so clearly proved.

Desire and anger washed through him in a confounding wave. Christ, one look at her and he'd lost control, succumbing to urges he didn't want to have—at least, not until his head was clear, and he could decide upon the future. Yet she'd snapped her fingers, and he'd gone running to her like a bloody trained hound.

He resented her power over him even as he hated the way he was treating her. It was a devilish conundrum, and one he didn't yet know how to resolve. But he also didn't want things to continue as they had been, tension hanging over them like a shroud.

More silence passed than he had intended, which he realized when Penny tugged her hand free as if she sensed the downward spiral of his mood. Her lashes lowered, she said, "I'll just go check on the boys—"

"They're fine." He caught her hand, tucked it firmly back into the crook of his arm. "Stay and walk with me a moment."

Doubt shadowed her gaze. "You want me to?"

"I asked, didn't I?" Hearing the curtness of his words, he strove for a calmer tone. "It's been a while since we've spoken alone."

She said nothing. She didn't have to seeing as he'd been the one to erect the wall of silence between them. Her bottom lip caught beneath her teeth; he didn't miss her cautious sidelong glance as they trudged on.

His mind latched onto a suitable topic. "How are the plans progressing for the Winter Ball?"

"Nicely." Some of her hesitation faded. "It's only been a week since I sent out invitations, and already I've received positive replies from nearly all. We'll have a crush on our hands."

This didn't surprise Marcus. Over the years, it had been a source of pride for him to watch Penny flourish in her role as the Marchioness of Blackwood. She'd tackled the job the way she seemed to do everything in life: with passion and verve, a willful determination to succeed. Through hard work (that she somehow made look easy), she'd become one of the *ton*'s most influential and fashionable hostesses... not to mention a doting mama and a mistress adored by all her servants.

Yet despite all her success, the confidence she'd earned by right, she'd never lost her vulnerability with him. After every glittering ball she threw, she'd always ask him, a hint of anxiety in her eyes, "What did you think, Marcus? Did you enjoy it?"

The knot tightened in his chest. How could he reconcile the loving wife who'd dedicated herself to pleasing him with the devious ex-spy who'd been lying to him for the entirety of their marriage?

He... couldn't. Perhaps it wasn't possible.

Enjoy the bloody walk. Don't think about it now.

Pushing aside his turmoil, he cleared his throat. "Who will we be expecting?" He asked not because he cared but because he wanted to prolong this domestic conversation. To linger for a little longer in this oasis of normality.

"The usual off-Season crowd: the Temples, Osterwicks, Knowles. Oh, the Hartefords will be there as well as Lady Helena is recuperating in Town."

"Recuperating?"

"From childbirth."

Marcus felt the resonance of sorrow and saw it in the trembling of his wife's lips. Despite the three years that had passed since they'd laid their stillborn child into the ground, the memory of loss quivered between them. It was yet another reminder of the intricate connections that bound them, invisible threads spun by time and shared experience. It flitted through his head that grief as well as joy could cement the bricks of a marriage.

"From what I hear, Lady Helena is doing well," Penny said quietly.

"I'm glad," he said.

Lord Nicholas and Lady Helena Harteford were more acquaintances than friends to them, but this was due mainly to the fact that the couple spent most of their time at their country estate. Whenever he and Penny did see the other pair, conversation flowed easily as they had much in common. Both couples had married around the same time and shared the experience of raising little hellions. Indeed, the Hartefords' three boys made James, Ethan, and Owen appear sedate by comparison.

"Girl?" he inquired.

Penny's lips curved wryly, and she shook her head.

"Poor Harteford," he said ruefully.

"Poor *Lady Harteford*. She's entirely outnumbered." His wife smiled at him.

At that moment, they walked into a patch of sun, the glow illuminating her. Diamonds of ice clung to her dark lashes. The ermine lining of her hood was no match for the downy perfection of her skin, the richness of her red coat setting off her vivid coloring.

God, but her beauty affected him, its impact as visceral as a fist in the gut. It had been this way from the start, and despite everything, he knew it would be this way until his dying breath.

Devil take it.

Tamping down the crazed urge to pull her into his arms, he cleared his throat, said gruffly, "Who else is coming?"

"I invited Carlisle as you requested. Both he and his brother Mr. Murray gave affirmative replies." A furrow formed between her brows. "Carlisle's not usually one for parties. I'm rather surprised that he agreed to come."

Marcus wasn't surprised. During his stay with his friend, it had become clear that there was only one way out of Carlisle's financial dilemma. As the viscount had cynically put it, "I've got a title to sell off, and I'll look for the highest bidder. It's a business arrangement pure and simple. As long as that's made clear, no reason marriage should interfere with my life."

The man had a lot to learn.

"Carlisle's turning over a new leaf," he said noncommittally. "Who else?"

"The Ashleys. Lady Cora most definitely and her husband possibly."

Marcus didn't miss the edge to his wife's tone. For some reason, she'd never liked the Countess of Ashley, in spite of the fact that *she* had been the one to lure Marcus away from the other —not that he'd needed much luring. One look at Penny had blinded him to other women. In the past, he'd secretly found his wife's possessiveness amusing and not a little arousing, but now it struck an unpleasant chord in him.

What did *she* have to be jealous about? He'd never carried on in secret with Cora or with anyone. He'd kept his vows, been honest and fully disclosing for the whole of his marriage—unlike his wife who'd lied about her past, about her other men.

Just like that, peace fled him. His shoulders bunched, his blood pumping hotly.

"Papa! Over here!" Jamie's voice penetrated his angry haze. His eldest son was waving at him, standing by the far edge of the park. "I think I've found a burrow of some sort. But I can't be sure what kind of animal made it."

Marcus drew a breath, glad for the interruption. "I'll be right there, son," he called. To Pandora, he said curtly, "I'll go see what he's found."

"Of course."

The hurt returned to her eyes, but he couldn't do a damn about it. Better to walk away than to let loose what was roiling inside him. He strode toward Jamie, fuming that the worst thing she'd done wasn't just betraying his trust. No, it was that she'd made him doubt *himself*.

He'd always been a man who'd known his own mind. Hell, he'd commanded an entire battalion, made snap decisions that had affected the lives of countless others, and never faltered. Never wavered. Since Pandora's revelations, however, his thoughts had been like a teeter-totter, going back and forth with galling ambivalence. His mood could shift wildly from one moment to the next, so much so that he thought he might be going mad.

He barely knew himself, and he hated it.

Shaking off his dour thoughts, he approached Jamie. "Now where's this burrow?"

"Right here, Papa." Jamie pointed excitedly at a hole in the snow by the base of a tree. "I think it may be a rabbit or possum—"

"Get down from there right this instant, Owen!"

Penny's urgent words made Marcus spin around. His heart rammed into his chest as he saw his youngest son balancing on the branch of an oak tree, some fifteen feet off the ground.

"But Mama I can walk just like Madame Magnifique," the boy sang, taking a step on the icy ledge. "Look at me—"

His words ended in a shriek as he lost his balance, tumbling, his arms flailing.

Marcus was already racing over, but Penny got there first, her arms outstretched. Their son plowed into her, and she took his full weight, falling backward with a thud. Her head hit the icy ground with a heart-halting crack.

He reached them the next second. With practiced swiftness learned on the battlefield, he ascertained that Owen was stunned but unharmed. He lifted the boy off Penny and parked him at his side, barking, "Stay here and don't move."

Owen nodded, his lips trembling. "Is Mama...?"

Pulse pounding, Marcus tore off his gloves and gently examined his wife. Her eyes were closed, but there was no blood. Nothing broken as far as he could tell. Her pulse was weak but steady.

"Penny, love," he said urgently. "Open your eyes."

Nothing. His gut clenched.

Pounding footsteps marked the arrival of Jamie and Ethan.

"Is Mama all right?" they blurted as one.

"She'll be fine." Hoarsely, Marcus said, "Wake up, Penny. You don't want the boys to worry, do you?"

An eternity seemed to pass before her lashes fluttered up, revealing dazed violet eyes.

Thank God. Thank bloody God.

"Owen...?" she whispered.

Marcus forced the words through the fierce constriction of his throat. "He's fine. It's you we have to worry about." With utmost care, he lifted her into his arms. "All right?"

"I'm fine. Just the wind... knocked out of me," she said, her voice breathless. "I can walk."

His heart knocking against his chest, Marcus carried her to the house, their sons following behind.

❧ 13 ❧

"Are you certain I can't get you anythin' else, milady?" Jenny said as she cleared away the breakfast tray. "Another pillow, more blankets—"

"I'm perfectly fine," Penny assured the ginger-haired maid. "There's no need to fuss."

"Well, you gave us a fright, you did, milady. All o' us. Waitin' for the doctor to finish with you last night, I ne'er saw the young masters so still and somber like. And 'is lordship nigh paced a trench in the drawing room."

Warmth unfurled in Penny's belly. "He was worried for me?"

"Beside 'imself, 'e was." Jenny smiled, her eyes brightening. "The kind o' worry that puts water 'neath the bridge, if you don't mind my saying."

Penny wasn't surprised that Jenny had noticed the rift between her and Marcus. After all, the maid was used to walking in and finding Marcus in Penny's bed. His absence and the tension between them outside the bedchamber must have caused speculation, and Penny wondered what the staff thought of the chill between master and mistress of the house.

"Is there much talk below stairs?" she asked.

Through the years, the maid's loyalty had proved unwavering. Penny trusted the other not only to be discreet but to tell her the truth. Jenny was worth her weight in gold.

"Some, milady," Jenny admitted, "but ev'ryone knows 'ow much the master dotes upon you, so most think it's a tiff. The kind that's part an' parcel o' any marriage. And like I said, 'is lordship's wearing out the carpet with 'is worry over you as we speak. 'E wouldn't do that if is 'eart weren't true, would 'e now?"

Hope flickered in Penny. "Thank you, Jenny. And I don't want the boys or my husband to worry, so please help me get dressed. The saffron wool, I think."

"But milady you ought to rest some more—"

An imperious rap on the door cut the maid off.

Penny's heart sped up. "Come in," she called, a trifle breathlessly.

Marcus strode in. He was in his shirtsleeves, his stark navy waistcoat molding to his lean torso, charcoal grey trousers hugging his muscular legs. The concern in his gaze stopped her breath altogether and made heat prickle behind her eyes.

She'd feared that he would never look at her this way again.

"Milord." Jenny dipped her knees. "I'll, um, just go get your toilette ready, milady." With a smile on her face, the maid scurried off and closed the door behind her.

The Ormulu clock ticked away on the mantel, Penny's heart even louder in her ears.

Wrapping a large hand around a poster at the end of the bed, Marcus said, "How are you feeling this morning?"

"Much better. I've a bit of a bump on my head, but mostly the blow I took was to my pride." She risked a smile. "I thought I could keep my balance."

"You caught our son falling out of a tree. You're lucky Owen didn't flatten you like a pancake."

"He has gotten bigger than I realized." Seeing Marcus' darkening expression, she added quickly, "It's not Owen's fault."

"Not his fault?" Marcus' scowl deepened. "The boy deserves a sound whipping for putting himself and you at risk."

The very idea made her bolt upright against the pillows. From the instant she'd held her firstborn in her arms, she'd vowed that no child of hers would know suffering, not if she could help it. No babe of hers would ever feel unsafe or unwanted or unloved. *Spare the rod, spoil the child* be damned.

Luckily, for the most part, Marcus deferred to her wishes. He was a stern disciplinarian, but his habit was to lecture and punish by means other than corporal.

"Owen's been punished enough. I'm sure he feels terribly about it," she insisted. "He doesn't need—"

"Devil and damn, woman, will you ever stop defending the little rogues?"

Marcus stalked to the side of the bed, staring down at her, his hands planted on his hips. Judging that he appeared more exasperated than angry, she decided to be honest. "No."

Her husband scowled. "He's losing his outdoor privileges for a month."

That was fair. "All right," she said softly.

"As for you..." He dragged a hand through his hair. "Damnit, Penny, don't risk your neck like that again."

"I'm sorry. I didn't think. I just saw him falling,"—she swallowed, flashing back to the panic, the utter horror of seeing Owen in danger—"and I reacted."

Marcus said nothing. She couldn't read his expression, didn't know if she'd pushed her luck, made him angry again. He surprised her by sitting on the edge of the bed.

"We should talk," he said.

Apprehension tickled her nape. "Yes?"

"The state of affairs between us. It can't go on like this," he said tersely.

Her stomach plunged. Had he come to a decision about their future? God, had he decided to divorce her after all—

"I can't forgive the past," he said in flat tones.

She couldn't breathe, couldn't even manage a nod. Terror paralyzed her.

"Thus, I believe the only solution is to move forward. To put it behind us," he went on. "For the sake of the children, we must turn over a new leaf and start afresh."

Slowly, her brain caught up. Sensation pierced her—relief so intense it was akin to pain.

"Would you be willing, Pandora?"

"Yes, Marcus, oh yes," she whispered.

"There are conditions," he warned. "First, after today, I don't want to hear about your past again. Knowing about your indiscretions,"—he bit the word out—"doesn't put me in a good place. So if there's anything else you've lied to me about, any other lovers, you'd best get it over with and tell me now. Because after today, I want to hear nothing of it."

There *were* secrets she hadn't revealed but not of the sort he was referring to. Not deceptions that she had to feel guilty about. She had the intuition that it was best to keep things simple.

"There've been no other indiscretions," she said quietly.

He gave her a level look. "All right then." He rose.

"That's it?" She couldn't keep the disappointment from her voice. "You're going?"

"You should rest."

"I feel fine. Trust me, I've taken far worse tumbles..." She trailed off, realizing what she'd inadvertently revealed. In her desire to keep Marcus with her awhile longer, she'd referred to her past. The past that he'd just stated that he wanted to know nothing about.

What in the blazes is the matter with me?

"There's more to discuss," she added lamely.

His brows winged, his arms crossing over his broad chest. "Is there?"

"About... us. Our arrangement." She felt as if she were

fumbling in the dark. "We haven't talked about what it means to start afresh."

"I believe we just did."

"Yes, I mean I understand that my past is behind us. But what about the future?" Swallowing, she said, "How are we to... to be... as a married couple, I mean?"

His expression didn't change. "You're referring to bedroom matters."

Blood rushed into her cheeks, but she whispered, "Yes."

After a moment, he said, "I owe you an apology."

"For what?" she said, confused.

"For the way I treated you in the bathing room."

Her cheeks heated further. Wetting her lips, she said, "That was my fault. I shouldn't have pushed you."

"No, you shouldn't have." He raked his hair again and then his hands planted on his lean hips. "But I shouldn't have left you as I did. I let anger get the best of me and treated you badly. It was wrong of me, and I apologize, Pandora."

"Apology accepted." Seeing his eyes soften, she blurted, "And it wasn't, um, bad. Only the way we parted. Before that, it was... wonderful."

His gaze went from warm to smoldering. "Goddamnit, Pandora."

"I know I've bungled things up, but since we're starting anew, I want to be a wife to you," she forged on. "I want to share a bed with you, be with you, because I lo—"

He placed a finger across her lips, stemming the tide of her words.

"Don't," he said sternly.

"Don't what?" she managed to say.

"Don't rush this. With time and effort, I think we can rebuild our marriage. But that doesn't mean that things will be as they were." His measured words tore through her, mangling her insides. "You mustn't push me on this or anything else. I will do my damnedest not to react badly, but I will not tolerate being manipulated."

Her heart knocked against her chest. "I'm not trying to manipulate you."

"For twelve years, you did," he said.

She had no rejoinder for that. None at all.

Because he was right.

Throat clogging, she said, "When can we... be together again?"

"Let me take the lead. We'll begin by rebuilding trust and go from there."

"All right." There wasn't anything else to say. Getting a second chance was more than she deserved, and she knew it. She wouldn't jeopardize the opportunity.

He cupped her jaw, and she leaned into the caress, desperate for the connection. She soaked in the strength and warm solidity of her husband's touch before his hand dropped away, and he took a step back.

"I'll send the boys up," he said. "They're eager to see you."

"They'll worry if they see me still in bed. I'll get dressed and go down to see them—"

"For God's sake, you just had a fall. Stay in bed for the day and rest, Penny."

Any further protests died on her lips. Her chest constricted, and she fought back the heat pushing behind her eyes. She was Penny again. His Penny.

She had that much back at least.

"All right, Marcus," she whispered.

He hesitated as if he was about to say something more... but instead he gave a curt nod and left the room. She sank back against the pillows and tried not to feel alone. To take comfort in the company of hope.

❧ 14 ❧

The next two weeks passed by in a blur for Penny. She had all the remaining details for the ball to take care of as well as a marriage to get back on track. With the former, she was confident of her progress; with the latter... not so much.

It wasn't that Marcus hadn't kept to his word. He didn't mention her past, and his manner toward her had noticeably thawed. Several nights ago, he'd even teased her at the supper table, asking her if she was trying to fatten him up by having all his favorite foods prepared. She'd wanted to roll her eyes because, unlike her, the man could eat like a bloody horse and not gain a single ounce. But, more to the point, he'd noticed her efforts to please him. This was progress, and it was good.

Yet all had not been smooth sailing. In the past, Marcus had been the even-tempered one in their marriage, the anchor to her occasional (or, more accurately, *not infrequent*) storms. He'd been her safe harbor, and he'd never been prone to moodiness or irritability. This new Marcus did have moods, however, and they were as changeable as the weather.

Whilst he kept his promise to not lash out at her, he would suddenly grow quiet, distant, his thoughts clearly occupying a dark and gloomy space. She hated his brooding, would prefer a full-fledged row over the tension that could set in at any moment like a deadly frost and wipe out their budding reconciliation. She felt as though she were a performer at Astley's, walking a tightrope no less treacherous than that of Madame Monique le Magnifique.

At the same time, she didn't dare to confront him. She'd given her word that she wouldn't push, and with their truce so new, she didn't want to drive them into conflict once more. Thus, she forced herself to bide her time and to let him dictate the pace of their rapprochement.

Yet a dangerous feeling was taking root inside her: impatience.

Just this morning, she'd received a note from Sister Agatha, a reply to her plea for counsel. Her old friend's advice had consisted of two words: *Be yourself.* But surely Agatha didn't mean Penny's *true* self.

Back when Penny had been Pompeia, the ruthless spy, she'd channeled her innate hotheadedness to her advantage. She'd been bold and daring, taking on perilous missions that others had declined. Since she hadn't had much to lose, she'd had little to fear. She'd thrown herself fully into any character that she was playing, nothing held back, and she'd played to win. Always.

Twelve years of marriage had tempered this part of her. She'd gotten accustomed to being Marcus' devoted marchioness, a role she'd chosen and, in truth, delighted in. So much so that it hadn't bothered her to suppress certain aspects of her old self because having Marcus' love—the love of the best man she'd ever known—was worth any price.

The fact was that she'd gotten so used to being Lady Blackwood that Pompeia had receded to a figure in the background. A dab of paint on a landscape. This had seemed a blessing since, in all honesty, she'd never liked Pompeia all that much anyway.

Yet now, for some inexplicable reason, that shadow of her former self was back and growing more prominent by the moment. 'Twas as if the spilling of her secrets had resurrected the Pompeia of old: a woman who would not be welcomed in any of the *ton*'s ballrooms. Who would not have the love of a man as decent and honorable as the Marquess of Blackwood.

But you don't have his blooming love now anyway, do you?

She blocked out the insidious inner voice, the one that had made itself more and more at home in her head. She didn't understand why now, after all this time, this unwelcome part of herself had come back. Perhaps the Spectre's reemergence had stirred up this hornet's nest. Whatever the cause, she vowed not to give into the hot, reckless impulses that Pompeia inevitably brought in her wake.

Pompeia, for instance, didn't want to abide by Marcus' dictate that they must take things slowly. That he should take the lead. No, Pompeia wanted to live by the adage, "Let bygones be bygones." And she wanted to do so by throwing open the door between their adjoining bedchambers, climbing into her lord's bed, and claiming what was rightfully hers.

So giving Pompeia free rein? Not an option.

To do so would destroy any chance of finding happiness with Marcus again.

Thus, Penny resolved to stick to her original plan. For two full weeks, she continued to behave as the good, properly contrite wife. And whilst Marcus did not visit her bed, he did at least stay home at nights. Pleasant bantering increased between them, some of their former camaraderie returning. They even passed an evening playing chess (in keeping with her penitent role, she let him win).

Now it was the evening of her much anticipated Winter Ball. 'Twas her chance to show Marcus that she was the perfect marchioness for him. And to show the world that the Blackwood Estrangement was over.

Inspecting herself in the cheval glass, she said, "You don't think the gown is too much, Jenny?"

"It's perfect," the maid declared. "Always said Madame Rousseau was the best modiste in all o' London, and she outdid 'erself this time. You're a masterpiece, milady: I han't seen anything 'alf so beautiful in all my life."

In commissioning her gown for the ball, Penny had told the modiste to spare no expense, and Madame Rousseau, being both an astute businesswoman and an artiste, had taken her at her word. The dress was constructed of pale ice blue silk, the fabric embellished with hand-sewn seed pearls to create the subtle, swirling effect of snow drifts. The bodice left Penny's shoulders bare, clinging to her bosom and waist, while the fashionably full skirts cascaded to her matching ice blue slippers.

The crowning achievement of the frock, in her opinion, was its element of surprise. From the front, the gown appeared quite modest; the décolletage, trimmed with a wide band of cerise ribbon, showed only the barest hint of her cleavage (no small feat given that she was rather generously endowed in this area). The other side of the garment, however, took a plunge, both literally and figuratively: it bared the smooth line of her spine, the bright red ribbon coming together in a perfect, elegant bow a hairs-breadth above the small of her back.

The dress was delicious... if a tad daring.

Penny straightened her shoulders. With Jenny's help, she'd cultivated a style of her own. As the Marchioness of Blackwood, she was known for taking risks when it came to fashion, and her bold style had always borne fruit. Marcus, for one, seemed to take special note of her more seductive gowns. Shivering, she couldn't count the times they had returned from an evening on the Town and barely made it to one of their bedchambers before he had her bodice pushed down to her waist, her skirts tossed up, his touch scorching and possessive...

You've tempted me all night, Penny, and now I get my just reward, he'd growl.

Blooming hell, there'd been times when they hadn't even made it back to the house. It was a private joke between them that Owen's lively temperament might be attributed to the fact that he'd been conceived during a rather bouncy carriage ride home from the Opera.

The memory of their prior after-party activities raised her hopes and bolstered her resolve. If everything went as planned tonight, she would have a smashing social success on her hands. Surely Marcus would be impressed by that. And maybe, just maybe, he might be inclined to extend the celebration to a private one of their own afterward...

One could always hope.

"The ruby necklace, milady?" Jenny asked.

She nodded, and the maid secured the heavy spangle of jewels around her neck. The collar of large blood-red rubies connected by cool, glittering diamonds had been a present from Marcus. He'd given it to her on the occasion of their tenth wedding anniversary.

For my wife, whose price is above rubies, he'd murmured in her ear.

Her throat thickened, her fingers brushing against the symbol of his esteem. The esteem she would win back, no matter what. She glanced in the mirror one last time and saw the battle light in her eyes.

"I'm ready," she said, lifting her chin.

If everything went as planned, tonight's ball would be the beginning of a fresh start.

Tossing back another glass of champagne, Marcus wished the bloody ball would end.

His gut tightened as he caught sight of Penny surrounded by a circle of admirers, four-fifths of them male. She was laughing, wearing a gown so indecent that it was all he could do not to stalk over and demand that she march upstairs to change. When he'd first watched her descending down the staircase to greet their arriving guests, he'd been struck anew by her loveliness, the juxtaposition of her cool beauty and passionate violet eyes causing his blood to rush.

Then she'd turned around, and his blood had plummeted to one part of his anatomy in particular. Lust bled into fury. Bloody hell, her entire backside was exposed.

By then, he couldn't do anything about it—at least, not without appearing like a jealous, lovesick husband. The very notion made him want to snarl. He wasn't going to give their damned guests a show, nor was he going to give Pandora the satisfaction of knowing that she could provoke him into acting like a fool.

If she wanted to display her charms in a manner worthy of a harlot, he thought grimly, then so be it. He would have words with her after the party. But if she made one untoward move tonight, if her behavior even edged toward impropriety... His hands balled at his sides.

"That's twice."

Carlisle's grim tones yanked him from his brooding. The viscount was standing next to him, watching dancers whirl by to a Scottish air, looking even less happy than Marcus felt.

"Twice?" Marcus said.

"Wick has danced with that damned chit two times," Carlisle clarified.

Marcus followed the direction of his friend's gaze.

Sure enough, Carlisle's younger brother, Wickham Murray, was cutting a swath through the dance floor. A great favorite of the ladies, Murray was a dashing Adonis type, his tall, muscular form clad in the latest fashion. Marcus recognized his present partner as Miss Violet Kent, younger sister to the Duchess of Strathaven. Murray and Miss Kent made a dashing pair. As Marcus watched, Murray led the dark-haired miss into a particularly energetic spin, their shared laughter eliciting looks from the others around them.

"Is there a problem with him dancing with Miss Kent?" Marcus said.

"Ten thousand of them, to be precise." Carlisle's features were set in foreboding lines. "My brother is in debt, and as I'm in no position to get him out of it, for once he'll have to take care of his own affairs. Which means he ought to be courting an heiress and not some middling class hoyden with aspirations to respectability."

Marcus noticed the whispers emanating from a gaggle of ladies posted by a nearby potted palm. Their fans beating the air in titillated synchrony, they were clearly taking note of and delighting in Carlisle's every word.

Lowering his voice—and hoping his friend would take the cue —Marcus said, "Miss Kent is quite respectable: she is the sister-in-law of a duke and a marquess."

"Unless her dowry exceeds twenty thousand—trust me, Wickham will need at least that much of a cushion—I don't care if she's related to the King himself." The viscount's lips curled in disdain. "Moreover, my brother needs a suitable wife to keep him in line, and I'm quite certain that chit,"—he cast a pointed glance at Miss Kent, who was flushed and laughing from yet another risqué spin—"can't even *spell* propriety, let alone put it into practice."

This time, gasps rose from the eavesdropping ladies, loud enough that they caught the viscount's attention. He narrowed his eyes at them, and they quickly waddled away, skirts rustling and palavering behind their fluttering fans.

"For a man averse to scandal," Marcus remarked dryly, "you've just provided enough fodder to satisfy the gossips for weeks."

"I was speaking the truth. If that's fodder, so be it." The viscount scowled. "This is precisely why I detest such social functions—no offense."

"None taken."

Especially since Marcus happened to be in agreement as it

pertained to this particular ball. His gaze honed in on Pandora once again, and the pressure in his veins shot up dangerously. The Earl of Edgecombe had joined her circle, and, as he did so, the bastard placed a hand on the small of her back.

Another man was *touching his wife.* The bugger's paw rested for an instant too long above the scarlet bow on her back—the one that beckoned like a gift to be unwrapped—before he removed it. Yet the damage was done. The scars flared on Marcus' brain: *Pierre Chenet, Jean-Philippe Martin, Vincent Barone.* Images of Penny being touched by those faceless others, moaning beneath them, made him burn beneath his collar. Savage instinct roared over him.

"You might want to rethink that." Carlisle gripped his arm, holding him back.

"He touched her." *They all did.* Rage quivered in his muscles.

"For only a moment, and Edgecomb would claim it was innocent. Now do you really wish to make a scene over a trifle like that? Do you want to appear like a jealous husband tied to your lady's apron strings?"

Carlisle's words penetrated his miasma of fury. It took everything he had, but Marcus willed himself to calm.

"I thought you said things were improved between the two of you," the viscount said.

Marcus pulled his jacket back into place. He wanted to punch something. Namely the face of the bastard standing next to his wife, peering down her blasted bodice. "They are."

"Right." The other's lips twisted. "This is why I'll never marry for love. Things may be good or they may be bad, but either way you wind up looking like a fool."

"You're not helping matters," Marcus said through his teeth.

"Of course I am. If it weren't for me, you'd be bashing in Edgecombe's skull, and trust me, the bastard's noggin doesn't need further damage. He's stupid enough as it is. Now you want my advice?"

"Do I have a choice?"

"Ignore her. Go be a host. You don't need to air your laundry in front of the entire *ton*."

Carlisle had a point. Expelling a breath, Marcus got himself back under control. *Carry on. Don't look like an idiot in front of the world.* He scanned the ballroom—and saw Lady Cora Ashley waving at him.

"You're right," he said. "Care to join me in greeting some guests?"

"No, thank you. I've seen all I can stomach for the evening." Bowing, Carlisle said, "Good luck and good night, my friend."

The viscount went one way and Marcus the other.

15

The ball was turning into a nightmare.

To make matters worse, Penny was at present cornered by her mama-in-law.

"You do have a way with parties," Lady Aileen, the dowager Marchioness of Blackwood, said. "This ball appears to be no exception."

The tiny, wrinkled lady waved the jeweled knob of her walking stick to indicate the winter wonderland Penny had spent weeks creating. Through the years, Penny had learned that success lay in the details, in setting a scene that contained the comfort of the familiar as well as the element of surprise. In this way, entertaining was not so very different from her work as an agent.

For tonight's event, she'd had evergreen branches and silver ribbons festooned across the high ceiling. Potted palms had been painted by hand to give the appearance of frost on the fronds, and icicles made of glass tinkled on the branches. The finest food and drink flowed freely.

"'Tis fortunate that my son's pockets are sufficiently deep to support your hobby," the dowager went on.

Penny had been waiting for the dig. As always, any compliment from the old harpy was double-edged. The passing years and the three grandsons Penny had produced had eased but not taken away the friction between her and Lady Aileen. Secretly, she suspected that the termagant was bored and enjoyed their feisty exchanges, and she, for her part, gave as good as she got. At times, this resulted in warfare, but overall the two managed to coexist without too much bloodshed. They did this for the sake of the man they both loved.

Swallowing, Penny snuck another peak at Marcus. Normally, the sight of him so starkly handsome in his formal wear elicited a tingle of feminine satisfaction, but tonight hurt and frustration bubbled inside her. She'd done her very best to please her husband... and he was acting like a blooming *ass*. He'd ignored her all evening and currently stood several yards away, entertaining a group of insipid ladies who hung upon his every word.

Cora Ashley was amongst them. Dressed in a delicate shade of pink, the blonde stood across from Marcus, batting her false eyelashes at him. As usual, her husband, the Earl of Ashley, was nowhere to be seen.

"What is going on between you and my son?"

The blunt words jerked Penny's attention back to the dowager, who was studying her with narrowed blue eyes that were a faded version of Marcus'.

"Nothing." Penny refused to give her mama-in-law the satisfaction.

"Utter claptrap. I may be old, but I am not stupid. In the past, Marcus never left your side for more than a half-hour at most, yet tonight he's acting as if he doesn't notice your existence." Before Penny could recover from the humiliating knowledge that Marcus' contempt of her was visible to all, Lady Aileen swept a glance over her from head to toe and announced, "It's the gown. Dear heavens, did you forget half of it upstairs? No man wishes his wife to be dressed like a strumpet, my dear."

Even as Penny's blood boiled, she kept a polite expression

pasted on her face. Her marriage with Marcus was none of the other's business. And the *last* thing she was going to do was take fashion advice from the dowager; the old mort wore her trademark black from head to toe, and if she traded her walking stick for a scythe, then the look would be complete.

Furthermore, not being an idiot, Penny didn't need her mama-in-law to point out that Marcus' behavior was due to her dress; his expression had grown as dark as thunderclouds when he saw the back of it. Or the lack of the back of it. But it had been too late for her to don another frock, and, moreover, it would fuel gossip amongst the guests if she ran off to change the very garment they were complimenting.

Thus, while Penny could admit that she'd made a miscalculation on her wardrobe choice, she couldn't stem her billowing anger. In the past, Marcus had liked her chic gowns, even if they were a bit daring. How was she supposed to know that his entire bleeding personality had changed? She couldn't read his mind, and instead of talking to her, he'd absented himself from her side all evening.

"Madame Rousseau assures me the gown is all the rage in Paris," Penny said.

Lady Aileen sniffed. "Yes, well, that says something about the French, doesn't it?"

"It says they have an excellent eye for fashion," Penny said through clenched teeth.

"And I have an excellent eye for my son's mood. If I were you, I'd go straight upstairs, my girl, and change into something more suitable."

If Penny had harbored even a spark of an inclination to change her dress, it was snuffed out by the fact that her mama-in-law had suggested it.

"I'm fine as I am." She drew her shoulders back.

"You shall reap what you sow. But don't say I didn't warn you.

The vultures,"—the dowager pointed her cane at the horde around Marcus—"are circling as we speak."

With that, she hobbled off to greet a circle of her cronies.

Penny's gaze went back to Marcus, still surrounded by ladies. The loathsome Lady Ashley was now not only batting her lashes at Marcus, she was also giving that annoyingly tinkling laugh at everything he said. Penny wanted to go over and tackle the trollop; good sense and her pride held her back.

"What a marvelous crush, Lady Blackwood!"

Tearing her attention away from Marcus and his harem, Penny focused on greeting the newcomers. The group consisted of four couples, all of whom she liked, so for the first time that evening, her smile felt genuine.

She first exchanged air kisses with Lady Helena Harteford. As usual, the beautiful, curvaceous brunette was accompanied by her tall, austere marquess, who bowed politely over Penny's hand. They were followed by Marianne and Ambrose Kent; the former's moon-kissed glamour was a direct contrast to her husband's lanky, salt-of-the-earth handsomeness, yet the pair went together like a fork and knife. The Duke and Duchess of Strathaven, a dark-haired and lively couple, said their hellos next, and then came Thea and her new husband Gabriel, the Marquess of Tremont.

Tremont inclined his tawny head. "Good evening, Lady Blackwood," he said.

Not long ago, mutual mistrust would have colored any exchange between Penny and her former colleague. First rule of espionage: trust no one—particularly another spy. But Tremont's recent marriage had changed him; the love of his marchioness had made him a different man, one whom Penny had trusted enough to join forces with. With the help of the Kents, Tremont and Penny had put an end to the affair of the Spectre and, in doing so, laid their past animosity to rest.

"I'm so glad to see you all here," Penny said and meant it.

"We've been here for a while," Thea confided, "but we didn't want to interfere with your hostess duties."

"What she means is that you were positively swarmed with admirers. We couldn't beat a path through to you," Marianne drawled.

"A problem I'm all too familiar with," Ambrose Kent muttered.

Being gorgeous and witty, Marianne Kent received her fair share of male attention. She winked at her husband. "You know I save all my waltzes for you, darling."

"Speaking of waltzes, has anyone seen Violet?" This came from Emma, who was craning her neck to get a view of the dance floor. "The minute she arrives at a ball, she's like a fish let loose in the ocean. I keep losing track of her."

"I don't see her, pet." Having the advantage of height, the Duke of Strathaven towered over his petite duchess, his pale green eyes alertly scanning the ballroom. "Could she be out in the garden?"

"Knowing Violet, she could be anywhere doing anything—which is precisely what I'm afraid of," Emma said, her brows knitting.

"Don't fret, love. We'll find her." Sliding a proprietary arm around his wife's waist, Strathaven said dryly to the group, "Excuse us while we attend to a domestic emergency," and the pair took off into the crowd.

"Should we help them look?" Thea asked.

"Tremont, Harteford, and I can go," Kent said. "You ladies enjoy yourselves."

As the men took leave of their wives, Penny suffered a stab of envy. Harteford murmured something in his lady's ear that made her cheeks turn pink, and Tremont kissed his new bride tenderly on the forehead. Whereas Penny's husband... she couldn't help but glance beneath her lashes in Marcus' direction. Blooming hell, he was *still* in Cora Ashley's group, only now the scheming bitch had wormed her way to his side. Penny gripped her lace fan as Lady Cora leaned up and whispered something in Marcus' ear, laying a pink glove on his arm.

On my *husband's arm.*

Fragile sticks snapped in Penny's hand.

"Is everything all right, my dear?"

Marianne's quiet words broke Penny's anguished reverie. For once, she felt too hurt and angry to measure her words. She didn't even have the heart to care about the presence of Lady Helena, who was a mere acquaintance. Seeing as the marchioness was Marianne's bosom friend, she probably knew some of the truth anyway.

"No." Bitterly, Penny tossed her broken fan into the pot of an adjacent palm. "Things are far from being right."

"Lord Blackwood must be proud of your event," Thea countered. "I've never been to a ball so beautifully planned, and no one can deny this is a crush."

This evening was supposed to be Penny's *piece de resistance.* Her way to win her husband back and show the world how much they loved each other. Instead, the entire affair was a fiasco.

"I thought this would help, but clearly it doesn't. None of this matters." She waved a weary hand at the roaring merriment. "He's still angry at me."

"Then why don't you go talk to him?" Marianne said. "Tell him how you feel."

"I don't know what is going on, and it's probably not my place to say." Lady Helena's soft, cultured voice broke in. "But if this has anything to do with husbandly problems, I might be able to help."

So Marianne hadn't said anything to her friend. Penny was grateful for the other's discretion. At the same time, she couldn't help but say wryly, "What would you know about those, Lady Helena? Your husband adores you and probably hasn't given you a moment's trouble."

Marianne and Lady Helena looked at each other—and burst into gales of laughter.

Penny frowned. "What is so amusing?"

Thea shrugged, her expression equally puzzled. "I haven't the faintest."

"Sorry—sorry," Lady Helena gasped, wiping her eyes with a handkerchief. When she was finished, she said, still smiling, "It's just that I *do* know a thing or two about troublesome husbands."

"Trust me, she does," Marianne said.

"And what I know leads me to believe that the gossip circulating about your estrangement can't possibly be true," Helena went on.

"Why would you say that?" Penny said with dull resignation. "Marcus hasn't paid me any attention all evening."

"But he *has* been paying you attention, my dear," Helena said, her eyes dancing. "He merely does so when you're not looking. Right now, for example."

Penny's head spun in Marcus' direction. Her gaze locked with his stormy one, and her heartbeat took off in a wild gallop. The next instant, he looked away, bending his head to catch something Cora had to say. A minute after that, he left the group.

To fetch something for the needy tart? Penny thought, outraged.

Jaw clenched, she said, "Why can't he just *talk* to me about what's gotten under his skin?"

"Because he's a gentleman," Marianne said. "When it comes to talking about their emotions, they'd rather have a tooth drawn."

"Or drink. Or pummel each other in the ring," Helena added.

"Or clam up—even though they are suffering inside." Thea's voice was gentle. "Being newly married myself, I can't profess to have the knowledge that you all do. But my mama always said there's one important adage to live by in marriage: to err is human —and to forgive, divine."

Flora would have said something similar.

"A wise woman, your mama," Helena said, nodding.

"I'll be the first to admit that holding out an olive branch is not my favorite activity, but when I've done it," Marianne said in philosophical tones, "it invariably works."

Given the disaster of the evening thus far, talking couldn't make things worse.

Penny heaved a sigh. "I'll go speak to him."

With impeccable timing, a footman walked past, and she snagged a flute of champagne from his tray. She swallowed first the bubbles and then her pride. After that, she went to look for her husband.

A quarter hour later, Penny approached the small balcony off the north end of the ballroom. The area was deserted as steaming new refreshments had just been brought out, luring the party-goers to the buffet tables. Marcus had not been amongst them. In fact, Penny had looked for him in all the obvious places, and he was nowhere to be found. As the servants hadn't recalled seeing him go upstairs, the balcony was the next likely place to search.

The thick burgundy drapes were drawn, the doors left open behind them. A cool draft shivered over Penny's skin. She pulled back one of the curtains... and her heart shot into her throat.

Marcus, standing in the cold moonlight.

He wasn't alone.

The scene ripped into Penny like a bayonet. Cora Ashley, in Marcus' arms, her mouth plastered to his. A jagged sound tore from Penny's throat. Marcus jerked, his head spinning in her direction, his gaze crashing into hers.

He pushed Cora away. "Penny—"

She didn't hear the rest. Insides splintering, she ran away—as fast and far as she could.

16

The next evening, Marcus made his way out of his club. He was drunk but not drunk enough. Guilt and self-recrimination swirled uneasily with the alcohol he'd imbibed as he waited for the footman to fetch his coat and hat.

Devil take it, what have I done?

He'd acted like a damned ass was what he'd done. He should never have agreed to meet bloody Cora Ashley on the balcony. When she'd begged him for a few minutes of his time, given him a teary-eyed Cheltenham Tragedy about her unhappy marriage, he ought to have told her to find another shoulder to cry on. But he hadn't. Why not?

Because he'd been so twisted up with jealousy and anger over Penny's past that he'd abandoned all good sense. Wallowing in righteous self-pity, he'd actually thought misery might make good company, and, as a result, he'd walked straight into an ambush. He hadn't set foot onto the balcony two minutes before Cora threw herself at him. The memory made his gut recoil. He'd shoved her away immediately—but not soon enough.

Penny had arrived at that moment, witnessing everything.

That shattered look on her face... His chest tightened, the knot so tight and painful he could hardly breathe.

He was a bastard through and through.

The footman arrived with his outerwear, and Marcus donned it, exiting into the wintry night. Snow was lightly falling, fat flakes that melted on his woolen greatcoat. He headed for his carriage just up the street, his thoughts whirling.

How am I going to fix this? He'd bungled things up so badly that he didn't even know where to begin. Last night, after the guests had left, he'd tried to talk to Penny, but she'd barred the door between them. The quiet, deadly steel in her voice as she told him to leave her be had been like nothing he'd ever heard from her—not in twelve years of marriage.

His head pounding with self-hatred, with too much champagne, he'd stumbled away, passing out in his bed. When he'd come to in the morning, he'd gone straight to Penny's chamber... only to find her already out. She hadn't left word where she was going or when she'd be back. He'd questioned her maid up and down until the woman looked on the verge of tears.

He'd waited all day at home for Penny to return but when dusk came, there was still no sign of her. Seeing the concern on his son's faces—probably because he'd worn a path into the Aubusson with his pacing—he'd read them a bedtime story and then took off himself to the club for a drink, unable to bear the agony of waiting any longer.

Of knowing how much he'd hurt Penny, the woman he loved more than his next breath, his cherished wife... whom he now realized he'd been punishing mercilessly. She might have betrayed him—but he'd more than returned the favor with his treatment of her. His throat thickened at the thought of her heartbroken, weeping alone somewhere; her pain was more than he could bear. He could only hope that he'd find her at home so that he could beg her forgiveness and ask her to truly start afresh with him.

He was prepared to let bygones be bygones and prayed that she felt the same.

Though the snow had stopped, the walk was slippery beneath his boots as he neared his carriage. The groom hopped down, hat pulled low and collar high against the falling snow, and opened the door for him.

"Cold night, eh, Harvey..." Marcus began.

He trailed off as he looked fully at the groom. Froze. It wasn't Harvey. Same mustache and brown hair but different eyes, glittering and long-lashed... At that instant, white powder clouded Marcus' vision. It filled his nose, his lungs, and, choking, he tumbled headlong into darkness.

❧ 17 ❧

1817

"What do you mean you're quitting? You can't quit," Octavian spat. "*Spies* don't quit."

"This one does." Pandora placed her palms on the spymaster's desk. Leaning forward, she looked him in the eyes. "I'm done, Octavian."

His beetled brows drew together—an expression that she'd learned meant a battle ahead. But it didn't matter. For the first time in her entire existence, she had something truly worth fighting for.

Octavian sat forward in his chair. "What about the others? Marius, Trajan, Cicero, and Tiberius are already on their way to the Spectre's lair in Normandy. They'll need your help to capture the villain once and for all: you cannot let your colleagues down."

After all these years, did he really think that he could guilt her into doing his bidding?

"We all joined this spy ring of our own volition. What the others choose to do is not my concern." She straightened from the desk but didn't break eye contact. "The only control I have is over my own destiny, and I choose to walk a different path."

Octavian shot to his feet, his wiry frame vibrating with suppressed hostility. He jabbed his index finger accusingly at her. "*You* do not get to choose. *I* made you, Pompeia. If I hadn't rescued you from the gutter, you'd be there still. Powerless. Broken. Have you forgotten what I did for you—how I gave you the weapons and will to survive?"

The dark alleyway swamped her. Sickly cologne mingling with sweat, weight pressing her down, vermin scuttling through the piles of rubbish. The flood of helpless terror: a lifetime of being careful, yet she'd fallen into a trap. No one to blame but herself. No one to help. No one to care. Her basket of blooms scattered and crushed over cobblestone, her screams muffled by leather, pain tearing into her...

When it was over, she lay there, curled on her side. A cool white wall sprung up in her mind, blocking out the fading footsteps. Her face smeared with wetness, her body numb, she reached toward a fallen violet, one that hadn't been trampled, her fingertips brushing petals that had somehow survived...

"I gave you power." Octavian's pale blue eyes pierced her through the fading memory. "Taught you how to avenge your honor and mete out justice. You *owe* me."

His words sliced but with the dullness of a blade much used. Her skin crawled but didn't break. Instead of blood, bitterness welled.

"I've repaid your *kindness* a hundred times over. I owe you nothing. I don't even owe you the courtesy of my resignation— but I'm giving it to you anyway." And because loyalty was difficult to die, even between spies, she said in low tones, "Call off the mission. Send word to Marius and the others. They'll need time to regroup and recalibrate their plan seeing as I won't be there."

"I'm not calling anything off," Octavian snarled, his fist pounding the desk.

His obstinacy shouldn't have surprised her. It had taken years, but she'd finally realized the truth: Octavian didn't care about her. He never had. Any pride or approval he'd expressed over the years had been that of a master praising a well-trained beast. The spymaster was ruled by ambition, by his obsessive need to hunt down enemy spies, and everything and everyone else—including the agents he'd trained—were just pawns in the game.

A game she refused to play any longer.

"Their blood's on your hands, then." She turned to leave.

"You think I don't know what this is about? You think I don't know about your little escapades at Toulouse and Quatre Bras?"

She froze, her heart thumping.

Octavian wasn't done. "You think I don't know about your pathetic attachment to Lieutenant- Colonel Marcus Harrington?"

Schooling her features, she faced the spymaster once more. "It's none of your business."

"It's my business when some damned army man takes away my best spy." His pale eyes narrowed, Octavian said, "Never thought you for a fool, girl."

"I'm not a fool," she said, her hands clenching at her sides.

"You are if you think a man like that will have anything to do with you. He's a blue blood and, what's more, a military man through and through. You and I both know that sort look down their noses at us, sneer at our methods even when they have us to thank for keeping their high and mighty selves alive. Risk your neck for his all you want, but he'll never thank you for it. And even if he could overlook the fact that you're an agent,"—Octavian's upper lip curled—"he won't overlook the fact that you're no genteel virgin. Men like him demand an expensive vintage, and they want to be the ones popping the cork."

The crude words made her swallow, but she forced herself to shut out the pain.

You have a plan. Marcus need never know the truth. You'll leave

Pompeia behind—become the woman of his dreams. You'll make him a husband and a father and give him everything he's ever wanted.

"I thank you for your insights on gentlemen," she said sardonically, "although, given the source, forgive me if I don't take them to heart."

"Damnit, Pompeia, you were born to this life." Like the master chess player he was, Octavian switched tactics with lightning speed. "Your place is here, not in blighted Society. I want happiness for you—and I can guarantee you will not find it with that sod Harrington."

"You think I'm *happy* here? With what I've done?" A harsh laugh scraped from her throat. "God, Octavian, you really have no idea, do you?"

Because he'd never given a damn about her—about anything other than his own ambition.

She turned and started walking.

Octavian's words followed her. "Marriage and love aren't for you, Pompeia. You're going to lose everything if you walk out that door."

"It's worth the risk." *Marcus is worth any risk.*

Yanking open the door, she walked out of the study and toward her future which, God willing, would include the love of a good man.

18

Awakening, Marcus blinked into the dark canopy above his bed. His first thought was that he had the devil of a head. His temples throbbed, and his mouth was drier than sandpaper. Remnants of some horror-ridden dream frayed the edges of his consciousness.

A nightmare.

It had been a long time since he'd had one. After the war, they'd plagued him, but they'd gradually gotten better with Penny sleeping by his side.

Penny. It all returned to him. What he'd done to her.

His stomach lurched, and this time it had nothing to do with the ungodly amount he'd imbibed and everything to do with the look of devastation on his wife's face. The look that would be branded upon his idiot brain until his dying day.

How could he have been such a bloody moron?

He lifted a hand to rub his face—and froze at the unexpected clinking. When he moved his arm, he heard it again. Metal against metal, like the links of a...

What the devil?

His eyes adjusting to the dimness, he saw with shock that a metal cuff circled his right wrist. Bolting upright, he yanked his arm, and shock gave way to disbelief when he discovered that a length of chain held him captive, securing him to one of the posters of his bed. Hold up, this wasn't his bed. What in the blazes...?

Shoving aside the thick bed hangings, he stumbled to his feet. Made it two steps before the chain pulled back, stopping him from getting any farther. Heart hammering, he scanned the dim room—a bedchamber. The hearth was lit, the flames giving off enough light to see the shape of a door at the far end of the room, shuttered windows along another wall. The place was oddly familiar, like a dream or a nightmare...

Fragments exploded in his brain. Shrapnel of what he'd thought had been dreams but which now took on the shape of... memories? White powder tasting of oblivion. A jolting carriage ride, his swaying consciousness, a hand brushing across his brow. *Sleep a while longer, my love.* More powder. Darkness.

"What in the devil is going on?" he snarled.

The door opened. The concentrated light of a single taper momentarily dazzled his pupils, but no way in hell could he mistake the woman holding it. Her raven tresses tumbled wild and free over her red satin dressing robe, and her eyes, glinting violet, locked with his.

"I see you're awake," his wife said.

───────────

Taking advantage of her husband's surprise, Penny set the tray down on the table between them. As she did so, the candle upon it flickered, chasing shadows over the room and Marcus' stern features. Her pulse raced. For once, he was unkempt: his hair was disheveled, a scruff emphasizing the hollows and hard edges of his face. His shirt was untucked and open at the collar, revealing the hard-carved ridges of his chest.

God, he was beautiful.

And furious.

Which was to be expected.

She stepped back, beyond his reach, and gestured to the tray. "I've brought you some refreshment. You must be hungry and thirsty."

"What the *hell* is going on?" His eyes blazed, his anger filling the room.

She wouldn't let herself get intimidated. She was beyond fear and, in truth, as angry as he was. The image of him kissing Cora Ashley scorched through her, bolstering her resolve.

Meeting his gaze squarely, she said, "What is going on is that I'm done with you steering our marriage. I agreed to let you take the lead because I'd wronged you and because you said it would help rebuild trust between us. Well, at the ball, your *method* of reestablishing trust,"—her voice quivered with emotion—"left much to be desired."

"That wasn't what it seemed," he said curtly.

"No? So I didn't witness you cozied up with Cora Ashley? You didn't have your arms around her? You weren't bleeding *kissing her?*"

"If you'll calm down—"

Oh no, he did *not* just say that to her. Her fury bubbled over. "I will *not* calm down. I may have betrayed your trust, Marcus, but I *never* betrayed our marriage vows. I've been faithful to you from the day we met. Which is more than you can say apparently."

"Goddamnit, woman, will you just listen?" He planted his hands on his lean hips, scowling when the movement caused the chain to clank. "She threw herself at me, all right? Took me off guard. I only agreed to meet her on the balcony because she said she needed someone to talk to. About her marriage."

Relief spread through Penny, but she said scornfully, "And clearly you're an expert on the topic."

"Pot calling the kettle black, is it? Seeing as *your* solution to our marital problems appears to be kidnapping."

"You're my husband. You belong with me." She said it as she felt it: unequivocally and with no apologies. "Not with some high-kick trollop who's no better than she ought to be."

Something flared in his eyes—and it wasn't just anger. She was suddenly aware of the tension sizzling between them, of the blood rushing hot beneath her skin. Her nipples were stiff and tingling beneath her robe.

"Yes, I'm your husband, Pandora. So bloody unchain me."

The command, the growl in his voice, aroused her even further. Her heart thumped when she saw that he was similarly affected: his erection butted the front of his shirt. But she couldn't give into desire—look at where that had got them in the bathing room. No, sex wasn't the answer to their problems... not all of them anyway. What they needed most was to talk, and, to do that, she had to keep a cool head. Which meant she needed to get away from her dangerous, bristling, irresistibly masculine husband.

She put more distance between them. Gestured to the tray on the table. "Refresh yourself. You'll need the energy for our talk. The talk we ought to have had in the first place instead of your asinine moratorium on communication."

"Wait one damned minute. Where are you going?"

"I'll be back after you eat and wash up." At the doorway, she paused, looking back at him. "You'll want to be comfortable while I tell you about my past."

To Marcus' disgust, he found he was ravenous. He polished off the meat pie and potato soup (favorites of his, although he probably should have checked for poison) and drank the entire pitcher of lemon-flavored water. After that, he took care of basic necessities behind the dressing screen and washed his face and brushed his teeth at the washstand. He couldn't remove his shirt with the manacle on, so he simply tore off the grubby linen and threw the soft woolen blanket (that Pandora had so *thoughtfully* left for him) around his shoulders. When all was said and done and he felt human once more, he found himself reassessing his situation.

And came to a rather startling conclusion.

His fury was fading, edged out by simmering, undeniable arousal. He didn't know if he wanted to throttle or make love to his wife—both, probably, and in equal measure. Mayhap at the same time.

Her shenanigans were beyond the pale—and he would make that clear in no uncertain terms when they had their little discussion. But he couldn't deny that her spirit and feminine fire aroused him to the point of madness. Truth be told, they always had. The way her violet eyes had flashed when she'd said that he was *her* husband and belonged here with her and the lengths she'd gone to carry out this crazed rendezvous at their cottage in the Cotswolds—oh yes, he'd recognized the place and the significance of it—made heat swell in his groin.

It was his Penny all over again.

Passionate, reckless, and seductive as hell, she'd captured his senses and his heart from the start—and nothing had changed that. Nothing *could* change that. Not her past, not his stupidity... not anything.

The realization broke over him like the first rays of dawn, shattering the darkness.

It had taken her abducting him to make him realize that he was already hers. As she was his. They belonged together, and the simplicity of that fact suddenly made the present tangled mess seem a hell of a lot less daunting. With his fog of anger and wounded pride finally burning away, he saw with crystal clarity:

what she'd done before their marriage didn't matter anymore. What did matter, however, was that she'd felt the need to lie to him all these years, and that was something they most definitely needed to address.

As her footsteps sounded in the hallway, anticipation licked up his spine. Damn, but he'd missed his Penny. His lips curved slowly. He didn't know what games she had in mind next, but whatever they were, he was more than willing to play.

19

Carrying a large box under her arm, Penny approached the door. She didn't know what to expect, and it didn't matter either way—because she was going to tell Marcus what he needed to know about her past. There was no putting it off, and doing so before had only worsened the state of affairs between them.

Taking a breath, she entered and saw Marcus sitting in the chair by the table. He'd eaten and washed up, thrown the blanket she'd left for him over his broad shoulders. Beneath the blanket, his chest was bare, the firelight flickering over the virile, hair-dusted ridges. He looked every inch the master of the house despite the fact that he was chained to the bed. She supposed she ought to unlock the cuff... then again, mayhap it was better to get matters off her chest *before* freeing him.

He rose at her entry, his impeccable manners almost amusing given the situation. That was one of the things she'd always loved about Marcus. He was a gentleman not merely by birth but by his behavior: he showed regard for others... even if they didn't deserve it.

"Feeling better?" she said.

"As good as a man who's been drugged and kidnapped by his wife can feel." His tone was neutral.

If he thought that would set off her conscience, he didn't know her. Didn't know the lengths she'd go to save their marriage. If being a spy had taught her anything, it was that sometimes the best choice was the lesser of two evils. Her arms tightened around the box.

"Would you care to have a seat?" Marcus gestured to the chair on the other side of the table, metal links rattling as he did so. "Or perhaps you'd prefer to unchain me first?"

She took the seat. It was the safer of the two options. Especially since she'd measured the length of the chain and knew she remained precisely ten inches out of his reach.

He followed suit, his posture in the chair lordly, his torso erect and his thighs slightly sprawled. She did her very best not to ogle his naked chest, the way the parted blanket accentuated the hard planes...

"You wanted to talk. So talk," he invited.

She didn't know what to make of his bland tone. Or his impassive expression. He didn't seem angry—but, if the past two months were any indication, it wouldn't take much to get him there.

Stop stalling. Get on with it.

Exhaling, she said, "I know you don't want to hear about my past, but you're going to have to. I've come to the conclusion that honesty is the only way for us to get past this."

"By all means then, be honest," he said.

What did he mean by having such a calm tone? His blue eyes were steady, and he seemed so much like her Marcus of old that she experienced the urge to just drop everything and crawl into his lap. To beg him to hold and cuddle her, to experience again the succor of being in his arms—the safest place she'd ever known.

Instead, she set the box on the table. It took up almost the entire surface. She put a hand on the lid before Marcus could lift it.

"We'll start at the beginning," she said. "The first time we met."

"You mean at the Pilkington Ball?"

In for a penny... "No, actually, that wasn't it."

A line formed between his brows. "I'm quite certain it was."

Deciding to let the truth speak for itself, she took the lid off the box.

Casting a puzzled glance at her, Marcus reached inside, parting the layers of protective tissue. He pulled out the jacket, examining the scarlet fabric, the insignia ... and incredulity shot across his features.

"What the devil? My officer's jacket. Why do you have...?"

She saw the moment that the truth hit him.

"It... it was *you*," he stammered. "The prostitute at the camp. The one who was being attacked by one of my men."

So he remembered her.

"Yes," she said.

"I don't understand. Why were you there?" His gaze suddenly sharpened. "Dear God, that night... Christmas. Starky was found dead. Natural causes by all appearances."

She wasn't surprised that Marcus made the connection so quickly. Lieutenant-Colonel Harrington was a brilliant man. She sent up a prayer that he'd believe her explanation.

"He was a traitor," she began.

"Yes, I know," he surprised her by saying. "Several months after his death, we came into possession of letters he'd written. Plans he'd drawn of our battle positions. The missives proved that he'd been selling military secrets to the French."

Relieved, she said, "Yes, he was."

Blue eyes bored into her. "Starky didn't have a heart attack?"

"No." She held her husband's gaze. "He didn't."

Marcus stared at her. Raked a hand through his hair. "By Jove... poison?"

She nodded, her heart an erratic presence in her chest. Not because she'd admitted to killing a turncoat—that bastard Starky had cost countless British lives by leaking information to the enemy—but because she didn't know what her husband would think of her. Of the fact that she was capable of taking a man's life.

"When Starky's betrayal came to light," Marcus said slowly, "Wellington declared that God had looked after us by taking a traitor from our midst. If Starky hadn't died when he did, he would have compromised us further, made the months leading up to Waterloo even more bloody and hellish. But it wasn't God's work." He sounded stunned. "It was you."

Penny wetted her dry lips. "Octavian said there was no other choice. Eliminate Starky or let innocents die in his stead."

"I understand his reasoning. I can even understand that actions during wartime are judged by a different set of morals than during times of peace. But what I don't understand," Marcus said, his voice low and dangerous, a muscle leaping in his jaw, "is why he'd send you—God, a mere *girl* at the time—to do such bloody, dangerous business!"

He was being protective... of her?

A lump rose in her throat. She didn't think it possible, but her love for this man grew even more. At the same time, she realized that he didn't quite grasp the entirety of what she was trying to communicate to him. Of what she was disclosing about who and what she'd been.

"Octavian sent me because I was one of the best." She said it without pride or emphasis; facts didn't require embellishment. "It wasn't my first of that sort of mission; it wasn't my last."

Marcus said nothing. His assessing gaze didn't leave her face. Perhaps the truth of whom he'd married was finally sinking in.

"Why did you keep it?"

His question was unexpected; it took her a moment to comprehend that he was referring to his jacket.

"Because I wanted to remember that night." In this, she had nothing to hide. "The night I fell in love."

His pupils darkened. "You didn't let on."

"How could I? For one, I was on a mission, and for another, I was disguised as a harlot. You would have turned me down flat."

He didn't refute her; they both knew it was true. He wasn't the type of man who'd stoop to consorting with a whore, to taking advantage of someone less fortunate than he.

"Why did you wait until the Pilkington Ball to approach me? That was nearly four years later," he said, frowning.

"At first, the business of Napoleon kept us both occupied. Then there was the aftermath of war to contend with. And I suppose the truth was,"—she shrugged—"I wasn't ready to meet you. I needed time to prepare myself, to become the sort of lady you might be interested in. Flora was helping me, giving me lessons in all the things a debutante ought to know."

"In between dispatching traitors and protecting your country, you were learning how to pour tea and make proper conversation?" Marcus said incredulously.

"Trust me, the former set of skills was far easier than the latter. I'd rather face a firing squad than a roomful of gossiping matrons."

He didn't respond to her attempt at levity. He said intently, "What if I had met someone else in the interim?"

She bit her lip before admitting, "I was keeping an eye on you."

One dark brow winged. "Define keeping an eye."

She released a breath. "I was there at Toulouse. In April of 1814."

Surprise rippled across his face. "That was a bloody fight. We were tasked with capturing the Heights of Calvinet, and I was lucky a sniper's bullet only grazed my..." His eyes widened, comprehension flaring in them. "It wasn't luck?"

"No," she said in a small voice. "It was such a fracas that I didn't see the sniper until too late. He got off the shot—although I did manage to alter the trajectory of his aim."

"Good God."

Not knowing what to make of his expression, she decided to forge on. "And I was there, in the village near Quatre Bras, two days before the battle. When that other sniper had you in his sights. But I got him in time."

"The bullet... it whizzed past my ear." Marcus wore a stupefied look.

Knowing her husband, she guessed that he might not be best pleased at the discovery that she'd taken an active role in keeping him alive. He was a proud man, not the kind to hide behind a woman's skirts. Or her pistol.

Sliding him a cautious glance, she decided she might as well get it over with. "After you left the army, I stayed apprised of your activities. I loved you, but I wasn't sure that I could win your love in return. When I heard the rumors that you were on the verge of offering for Cora Pilkington, however, I knew I had to act. I gave Octavian my resignation and came to London to find you."

Silence fell. His eyes were hooded, his features carved from granite. She gathered her courage to face the darkest of her sins— the men she'd bedded—but Marcus spoke first.

"Come here." He rose to his feet.

Her heart beat madly at the blazing heat of his eyes. How angry was he at her? Would he let her finish what she had to say?

"I'm not done." She drew a breath, squared her shoulders. "I... I have to tell you about... Pierre Chenet, Jean-Philippe Martin." She had to force out the last. "Vincent Barone."

"I don't give a damn about them," he stated. "They don't matter."

"They... don't?" She stared at him, confused.

"I realized that after the Winter Ball. After I acted like a bloody fool, nearly bungling our marriage beyond repair, I realized that nothing matters but us being together."

"But I thought... you... you said that things could never be the same between us. That you couldn't forgive me," she stammered.

"Can *you* forgive *me* for being an imbecile where Cora Ashley is concerned?" he returned.

"Yes," she whispered.

"Then I can forgive you for the past. For things that were done before we were even together." The flames in his blue eyes mesmerized her. "Now get your pretty arse over here."

Her nipples tingled, but she held onto her remaining ounce of self-preservation. "Why?"

"Come here, and you'll find out."

It was a risk, she knew, but she couldn't resist the command in his voice, the smolder in his gaze. She rose, closing the distance between them, taking those last ten inches into uncertain territory. She was a woman who'd stared death in the face more than once and run away laughing, and yet now she trembled as she stood before her husband.

He curled a big finger under her chin, tipping it up, and the tenderness that softened his hawkish features made her eyes sting.

"Pompeia, Pandora Smith or Hudson, whatever you choose to call yourself—I have loved you from the moment we met. Or, I should say, from the first time you revealed yourself to me. I have loved you every moment since, and I will love you," he said solemnly, "until my dying breath and beyond. Because you are my lucky Penny, my wife, the other half of my soul."

A sob worked its way up her throat; overwhelming joy and relief prevented her from speaking.

As it turned out, she didn't have to. In the next moment, his mouth claimed hers in a kiss more eloquent than any words.

Marcus swung his wife up into his arms and carried her to the bed.

With one knee on the mattress, he gazed down at her like the treasure that she was. Humbled by her beauty and strength and the fact that she'd pledged both so steadfastly to him, he cupped her soft cheek and whispered, "I always knew you were an angel. I just had no idea you were my own Guardian Angel."

She flushed. "That's doing it a bit brown. I just... lent a hand. When I could."

"Darling, *lending a hand* is helping with my cufflinks. Adjusting my cravat. What you did at Toulouse and before Quatre Bras..." He shook his head, unable to express the feeling burgeoning in his chest. It was too much, too large to put into words.

"It doesn't disgust you?" she whispered. "To know that I'm... capable of killing?"

There it was. That complexity of hers that had captivated him from the start. Mystery combined with candor, sultry confidence mingling with the sweetest vulnerability.

"Did you kill indiscriminately?" he said.

She shook her head.

"Murder innocents, babes in their beds?"

Again, her head rocked against the mattress.

"Then to know that you've killed turncoats and enemies of our nation? That you would kill to save my life?" Bending down, he brushed his lips against hers. "No, my love, it doesn't disgust me."

"I would do anything for you," she said.

There was no hesitation, no shame in her words or the lush depths of her eyes. He couldn't help but marvel at the woman he now knew her to be. She'd survived such darkness in her life, yet her love... it had always been clean and pure. The truest thing he'd known.

"God, I adore you," he said roughly and possessed her mouth once more.

He'd intended to take things slowly, to make up for his stupidity and the weeks they'd lost because of it by making sweet and gentle love to his lady. But when her lips parted, her tongue luring him inside, he knew this would be no sedate reunion. The kiss caught fire, heat searing his insides, and before he knew it they were tearing at each other's clothes, fighting to get rid of anything between them.

"The chain," she gasped. "The key's in... the other room..."

"Damn the chain. There's no escape for me or for you, my love. Not from the start. Not ever." He tossed her robe over the side of the bed. "And now I have you exactly where I want you."

Hunger reared in him at the bountiful feast that was his wife. Kneeling at her side, he dove right in, manners be damned, latching onto her sweet tits. Jasmine and neroli ignited his senses, his blood running hot and fast as he suckled her nipples, wetting them in turn, rubbing and playing with those decadent rosebuds while she panted his name.

His gluttony led him farther down, his tongue tracing the grooves of her ribs, the sultry indentation of her belly. His mouth watering, he clamped his hands on her white thighs, spreading

them wide, and paused to gaze at her pussy. To admire the delicate ebony thatch and the peekaboo view of dewy pink flesh
beneath.

Lust pounded in his head, his heart, his cock.

"Damn, I've missed you," he muttered.

Too impatient to maneuver himself between her thighs, he
simply swooped down and buried his head where he wanted it.
The view was topsy-turvy, but being well acquainted with his
wife's lovely quim, he figured he knew his way around from any
angle. He parted her folds, swiping his tongue into her honeypot,
desire roaring through him as he lapped at her sweetness. Behind
him, he heard her panted moans, and he doubled his efforts,
exposing her peak, flicking the center of her pleasure in rhythm
to his own thundering heartbeat.

Just when he thought things couldn't get better, her hand
circled his throbbing cock. She fisted him, tugging with just the
right pressure to drive him mad. As he sought to return the favor
of exquisite torture, she suddenly shifted, her head nudging
beneath him and between his legs. He bit off a curse when her lips
closed around his throbbing cockhead.

"Christ, Penny," he groaned.

She'd pleasured him with her mouth in the past—and he'd
always loved it, considered it a decadent treat. But this position
was new for them. New and unquestionably erotic.

"Damn, I've missed you."

Her throaty voice, throwing his own words back at him, sent a
hot quiver up his spine. And that was before she got busy trying
to cram as much of his cock as she could into her mouth. His hips
moved, unable to resist the sweet and generous lure. He plunged
deeply, groaning as he simultaneously buried his erection in her
throat and his mouth in her cunny. The sound of her muffled
moan, the feel of it vibrating against his turgid shaft, brought him
right to the edge.

But he wouldn't go over, not without her. He tongued her

proud bud, working two fingers into her sheath at the same time. Her slick muscles clutched at his pumping touch, and when he felt her panting against his cock, unable to focus on what she was doing, he judged that she was there. Lost in the raw pleasure. He suckled her pearl, and she bucked against his mouth.

Gorgeous and wild. His Penny. All his.

In the next breath, he shifted direction. He was on top of her, face to face, front to front, the tip of his cock lodging against her soft, wet entrance. Looking into his beloved's heavy-lidded eyes, her flushed face, he thrust himself home. Heat—lush and wet. Fire raced up his spine, incinerating his self-control. He drove into her, deep and deeper, and she responded by circling his hips with her legs, giving him more access. Giving him everything.

"God, that's good," he growled.

"Yes, my love. *Yes.*"

Her lips parted, and he took her mouth the way he was taking her pussy: hot and hard, nothing held back. Nothing but the joy of being how they were meant to be. Together, loving.

Her body heaved against his in perfect counterpoint. Soft against hard, sweat glazing their skin and heightening their closeness. Pressure burgeoned in his stones as they slapped rhythmically against her giving flesh. He was barreling toward his climax, and this time there was no stopping it. But he knew his wife and knew how he wanted to go over.

"Come again, Penny," he grated out. "Take me with you."

"Oh, Marcus, *yes*—"

The first spasm of her pussy made his neck arch. Groaning, he pounded into her, her passage wringing his length and demanding his bliss. Heat exploded from his balls, his seed boiling up his shaft and jetting from him in luxurious torrents. Even after the shudders faded, he couldn't stop pumping into her, continuing to claim her with gentle strokes.

Looking into his wife's sated eyes, he murmured, "How was that for making up?"

"Not bad." Her lips curved in a saucy smile. "For a start."

"You're going to kill me, you know."

He said this with a grin—because he couldn't wait.

Penny woke slowly from a deep and luscious dream.

Only it wasn't a dream.

Looking into Marcus' warm blue eyes, his fingers sifting through her hair as she lay on her side facing him, she felt joy pervade every cell of her being. She had her husband back. After they'd made love last night, she'd fetched the key to free him, and he'd made love to her again, slowly and tenderly, before they'd fallen asleep in each other's arms.

And he was still here.

"Good morning, love," he murmured.

"Yes, it is," she whispered.

His lips tipped up, the smile reaching his eyes. "Thanks to you and your exceptional execution of this rendezvous. I still can't believe you pulled this together in a day."

It *had* been a rather large feat. She'd spent the day after the disastrous ball running about, making frantic arrangements. She'd sent word to have the cottage readied and supplies stocked. Then she'd made excuses to the children, telling them she was accompanying Papa on a business trip; she'd also arranged for their care during her absence. After that, she'd dashed a note off to Flora, asking for prayers that all would turn out well. Oh, and she'd had to visit a certain establishment in the rookery to obtain the drugging powder.

"It was worth it," she told him.

He continued to stroke her hair. "How long do we get to stay here?"

"A week." God, she loved his touch. "Your mama agreed to look after the children."

"You asked Mama for a favor?" His smile turned wicked. "By Jove, you *were* desperate to get me back."

She had been. Desperate enough to go to the dowager with hat in hand. That didn't mean, however, that she'd revealed the true reason why she'd needed the other's assistance. *I'm going to kidnap your son in order to fix my marriage* just didn't quite have the right ring. Thus, she'd given her mama-in-law the same explanation she'd given the children.

A business trip, eh? Well, you two enjoy yourselves, Lady Aileen had said grandly. *I'll have the household and children straightened out and in ship shape by the time you return.*

At the time, Penny had been so grateful for her mama-in-law's help that she'd overlooked the snide comment on her house-keeping and parenting skills.

Now she rolled her eyes at Marcus. "Don't get all bigheaded about it." She lifted a hand, intending to slap him playfully on the chest—and froze at the rattling of metal, the weight around her wrist. With disbelief, she saw the manacle and chain securing her to the bedpost.

"What in heavens?" she said indignantly. "Release me this instant—"

She broke off with a gasp when Marcus flipped her onto her stomach in a swift move. He drew her hair off her shoulders, and she shivered as his lips brushed the sensitive skin of her nape before moving up to her ear.

"What's sauce for the gander." His hot, husky voice held a catch of laughter.

Then he was kissing down the length of her spine, gnawing and licking. Her cheek against the mattress, Penny gave up any pretense of resistance. *Fair is fair, after all*, she thought philosophically. Then she gave up thinking all together. Her lusty sigh turned into a moan as her husband proceeded to show her his spicy and exceedingly delicious version of sauce.

BLACKWOOD COUNTRY SEAT, 1826

"Go, son. Be with your wife. I'll see the children back to the house."

Marcus took his gaze from Penny and looked at his mama. Beneath the brim of her black bonnet, she wore her usual stoic mask, but he saw the worry in her faded eyes. The dowager might have a reputation for being a harridan, but those she loved, she loved deeply. And through the years, he knew that she had come to love Penny, even though the two of them butted heads on a constant basis.

Marcus placed a hand on his mama's shoulder, feeling the frailty beneath the black velvet. "Thank you, Mama. We'll be along soon."

"Take your time. And Blackwood... you'll have a care, won't you? These things affect ladies differently than gentlemen. You give life to something, and seeing its flame extinguish,"—her voice wavered a little, and he knew she was thinking of James, the son she'd lost—"it's not easy, my boy. Not easy at all."

After seeing his mama and the boys off in the carriage, Marcus headed over to his wife.

Penny stood beneath the graceful, curving branches of a maple. Her black gown and her own dark coloring made her stand out against the burnished brightness of the leaves, but she looked pale and wan. When she lifted her gaze to his, a pang resonated in his chest. Bewilderment and pain. The throbbing ache of a wound only three days old.

Quietly, he said, "Mama's taking the boys for a while. We can stay here as long as you want."

She nodded dully, her gaze returning to the small marble headstone. A wreath of pink flowers that she'd made lay against it. He stood by her side, for once uncertain what to say or do. How to give comfort when there was none to give.

Her low voice broke the silence. "Do you know," she said, "I overheard one of the villagers gossiping when I went to buy the flowers."

"Gossiping about what?" he said, frowning.

"One of them was saying what a lot of fuss was being made over a stillborn babe. She said that this happens all the time in the village, and here we are acting as if the sky has fallen."

Fury ignited, roaring through him. "Do you know who it was?"

"She was just speaking her mind." Penny drew a wobbly breath. "But it did make me think: why *do* babes have to die? Why did our little girl,"—her voice hitched—"have to die?"

Her question twisted his gut. All he could say was, "I don't know."

"Do you think it could be punishment... for past wrongs, sins I've committed?"

"God, no," he said, appalled. "Of course not. How could you think such a thing?"

"Sometimes I wonder about it. If I had been a better person, led a more sinless existence—"

"Penny, look at me." He lifted her chin, the sheen in her violet eyes tearing the scab off, making the wound bleed anew. He said firmly, "One has nothing to do with the other. Life is mysterious. Bad things happen for no reason at all."

"You don't know that," she whispered. "Flora—my mama, I mean—she had a saying. *As you sow, so shall you reap.*"

Shadows angled through her gaze, her lashes wet and spiky. He didn't know what she was thinking, but he forged on heedlessly, driven by the need to slay any pointless, needless guilt that she might be feeling.

"Even if that were true, you'd have nothing to worry about. You're a lady, sweet and pure. What wrongdoing could you have possibly committed?" He tucked a fallen curl behind her ear and felt her tremble. "If we were to be judged by our sins, between the two of us, surely I'd be the one most deserving of punishment."

"That's not true. You're a hero," she said in a scratchy voice.

"During the war, I committed atrocities. So many of them. You know—you've witnessed my nightmares." He brushed his knuckles against her cheek. "I wish to hell that I hadn't done those things, but there's no changing the past. I did what I did in the name of duty, and I have to live with it. But it has nothing to do with our little girl dying."

"Your actions were honorable. You protected your country." She touched his arm. "Marcus, you're the finest man I've ever known."

"And you, my love, are the finest woman I've ever known. You're a doting mama to three healthy boys and a loving wife to me. You've given us the gift of happiness and love. Surely that must erase whatever sins you think you may have committed," he said tenderly.

Her lips quivered. A tear slipped from the corner of her right eye.

He gathered her in his arms and held her against him while sobs shuddered through her. His own eyes heated, prickling with wetness.

Even after the storm passed, they stood together for a long while. With leaves shedding around them, he tightened his hold on his wife as they kept vigil with the angel who had passed all too fleetingly through their lives.

Finally, he said, "It's getting cold. We should go inside."

Penny nodded, and he took her hand, intending to lead her away.

"Marcus."

He turned his head to her, giving her an inquisitive look. "Yes, love?"

"I just wanted to say... I still don't know why this had to happen. And I haven't made my peace with it." Her eyes were very bright. "But I'm glad that you are here with me."

His chest clenched, his grip on her hand even stronger. "I'll always be here, Penny. That's what marriage is. Being together through every season, no matter what it brings."

Her smile was small and tremulous. Her fingers squeezed his.

Together, they made their way back home.

❧ 22 ❧

DECEMBER 1829

For Penny, the time at the cottage proved to be a second wedding trip. The husband she adored was back and, truth be told, things between them were better than ever. And she wasn't thinking just of the lovemaking (of which there were several daily episodes, each time different and creative, and *all* of it sublime).

She hadn't realized just how much her secrets had burdened her through the years, weighing her down like a water-logged coat. Shedding the past made her feel freer than she ever had in her marriage. That Marcus could accept the things she'd done as a spy... she hadn't known how important that was. 'Twas as if her soul had been corseted all this time, and now the strings were loosening, allowing her to breathe more fully.

True, her one despicable secret remained... but since Marcus had said the past didn't matter, she'd decided to let that sleeping dog lie. She wasn't about to reveal her dishonor when she didn't have to. If this decision made her lily-livered, then so be it. She'd rather be a coward with a husband who loved her than a brave fool who'd risk losing everything she'd just won back.

She told herself that things were already better than ever between them. No need to gild the lily and risk mucking everything up in the process. No, best to leave things as they were. After all, Marcus had forgiven her, didn't condemn her for her sins. She no longer had to constantly fear exposing herself and could give freer rein to her impulses. In fact, her husband seemed to delight in it when she did.

On just such a whim, she suggested they take a walk on the third day. Marcus at first balked, preferring the cozy warmth of the cottage and, waggling his brows, offered up a naughty alternative to braving the outdoors. But seeing as she could still feel the tingling aftermath between her thighs from their bout before breakfast, she was able to remain steadfast in her plan to get them some fresh air and exercise.

Thus, a half-hour later, she found herself walking hand in hand with her spouse through the woods surrounding their property. The bright afternoon sun sparkled off the ice-crusted branches and untouched fields, its warmth making their fur-trimmed hats and gloves almost unnecessary.

Breathing in the crisp air, she said, "See? I told you it wasn't too cold for a walk."

"Perhaps not for you, you hot-blooded wench." Marcus' eyes, as blue as the clear sky, smiled at her. "But some of us prefer lounging in front of the fire over freezing our arses off."

"We lounged in front of the fire all day yesterday."

"Yes, and what splendid lounging that was."

Seeing as how they'd both been naked, their limbs entangled and other body parts joined as well, she couldn't disagree.

"I don't recall you being quite this randy before, Lord Blackwood," she teased.

He stopped, turning to her and curling a gloved finger beneath her chin. "I've always wanted you, Lady Blackwood. It took almost losing you to realize how much."

Her throat clogged. Blooming hell, she loved this man.

He touched his mouth to hers, and they walked on. The light covering of snow crunched beneath their boots, and seeing the pair of tracks they left behind them on the unblemished white canvas made her feel as if they were the only two people on earth... at least for the next few days. They reached the edge of a small pond, and she looked out onto the tranquil surface, content-ment bobbing within her.

"Penny, there's something I've been wondering about."

"Hmm?" Her gaze caught on a lone bird floating on the water. No other birds nearby. Brave thing, taking on the elements alone.

"Did I make you feel like you needed to lie about your past?"

Her eyes flew sharply to Marcus' face, and seeing his furrowed brow, peace fled her. She'd thought they'd agreed to put her past behind them. Had he changed his mind already? "I beg your pardon?" she said.

"No, love, don't look worried. I meant what I said: what you did before our marriage doesn't matter to me." The earnestness of his gaze anchored her. "But our relationship does matter, and I want to know if there was anything about *me*—anything that I could or should have done—that would have made you confide in me earlier."

Her pulse steadied. She shook her head. "It wasn't anything about you, Marcus. You're the most trustworthy, honorable man I've ever met. That's why I fell in love with you in the first place."

"It wasn't my Adonis-like looks?" He quirked a brow.

"Well, that too." Knowing that he was trying to lighten the conversation and make it go more easily for her, she dug up as much of the truth as she could. "Growing up as I did, I learned that survival depended on trusting no one. My training as an agent honed that instinct. Then I met you, and suddenly my whole world seemed topsy-turvy. I wanted things I didn't think were possible for a woman like me."

He studied her, said quietly, "A woman like you?"

As always, she felt bared by his intense gaze, those vivid blue eyes penetrating all her layers... down to the ugly core. She swallowed her sudden panic. "A spy, I mean. Someone who'd done terrible things—even if they were done in the name of justice."

"Penny, you are the sweetest, bravest, and strongest woman I know."

His praise flooded her like sunshine, chasing away some of her shadows, but she said truthfully, "I'm not sweet."

"To me, you are." He cupped her cheek, warm leather against her cool skin. "Knowing what I do now about what you survived and the world you came from only makes me marvel more at the sweetness of your love. I don't know how you endured such harshness to become the woman that you are. I only know that by some miracle you're mine."

Her vision blurred. "Don't make me cry. My lashes will freeze together."

"I have no intention of making you cry ever again—unless those tears are ones of joy. But I want you to know that you can talk to me about the past... about anything." His thumb traced the slope of her cheekbone. "I want you to know that you can trust me."

The moment hung between them like their puffing breaths. She felt the albatross of shame hanging around her neck and wanted to free herself, yet it tightened like a noose. Fear choked her, the memory of being powerless, the pain, the feeling that she would never be clean again. And, worst of all, there was the fear of losing him.

Perhaps Octavian had been right after all. *You can take a girl from the gutter but not the gutter from the girl.* She'd come a long way, yes, but she'd never be able to stop looking back. Not completely. And she wouldn't burden Marcus with her disgrace.

"I do trust you," she whispered.

But I don't trust myself. I don't trust that I'm good enough for you.

His eyes searched hers. "All right, love," he said finally.

She was relieved when he let the matter drop. They continued on their walk, their conversation turning to lighter topics as they completed the loop around the pond. By the time they headed back toward the cottage, her mood had lifted again. Their banter had grown downright flirtatious. She was giggling, dodging his playful hands, as they approached their love nest.

The laughter stuck in her throat when she saw a rustic horse-drawn wagon by the cabin. Pushing aside a pile of blankets, a woman wearing a plain grey coat descended from the driver's seat. Although twelve years had passed since Penny had last seen that gentle face and those warm brown eyes, it suddenly felt like only yesterday. With a cry, she ran forward, slipping a little in the snow, and threw her arms around her friend.

"Flora," she said breathlessly. "What are you doing here?"

"I received your note, and I had to come make sure you were all right." Flora's gaze went to Marcus, who remained at a respectful distance, his expression curious. "If need be," she said in a low voice, "I was going to pretend that I was a stranger lost in the woods who just happened by your cottage."

"You don't have to pretend. I told Marcus about you... although he doesn't know that you're alive," Penny said, her tone equally soft.

"Did you tell him everything about your past?" Flora whispered.

Penny bit her lip. "Most everything."

Understanding rippled through Flora's eyes. She said quietly, "The troubles between you, my dear—are they patched up?"

"Yes. He's forgiven me for deceiving him." Expelling a breath, Penny smiled and linked her arm with her friend's. "Come and meet him. I think you'll approve."

"If he loves you the way you deserve, I already do," Flora said.

If learning that Flora Hudson was still alive and now administered to the needy as Sister Agatha came as a surprise to Marcus, then *seeing* Penny with Agatha proved a revelation. He'd witnessed his wife occupying many roles: doting mama, loving wife, caring mistress, glittering society hostess... she was a woman who could do anything she put her mind to. Yet he didn't think he'd ever seen this relaxed and youthful side of her.

Her joy was childlike, contagious, giving him a glimpse of the vulnerable, sweet girl she might have once been. The one that Agatha had clearly had a hand in raising. For it was clear to him that Penny and Agatha were kin, even if they didn't share blood. And he was filled with profound gratitude for this lady who'd clearly taken his Penny under her wing.

Sister Agatha was soft-spoken, pious, a handsome woman who had aged with indifferent grace. It was difficult to fathom that the lady had once been a spy. When she spoke about her charitable works through the Society of St. Margery, located some half-day's ride from the cottage, however, her eyes lit with her strength of will. The kind of tenacity and passion he'd seen on his wife's face when she took up a task, be it tackling some knotty household problem or planning her next society event or even fighting for their marriage.

Yes, he owed a debt to Sister Agatha.

After they finished supper—a delicious stew that Penny had made, surprising him yet again with her hidden culinary skills (was there anything the woman couldn't do?)—they continued chatting in front of the fire. Agatha took the armchair closest to the hearth, whilst he and Penny shared the snug love seat opposite.

"I cannot wait for you to meet the boys," Penny was saying. "They will adore you."

"I've heard so much about James, Ethan, and Owen that I feel as if I know them already." Agatha turned warm yet astute brown eyes upon him. "Though for reasons of necessity Pandora wrote infrequently, she never spared the superlatives when describing your children, my lord."

"When it comes to our offspring, my wife wears rose-colored lenses." He winked at Penny. "Don't believe a word she says, Sister Agatha. She'll have you believing the rascals are angels, complete with halos and wings."

"She used even more superlatives when describing you," Agatha said.

"I take them all back." Penny narrowed her gorgeous eyes at him. "Our boys are *not* rascals—they're merely high-spirited."

"She means this literally," Marcus told his wife's friend. "Owen's spirit recently moved him to scale fifteen feet up a tree, quashing Penny on the way down."

Agatha looked like she was fighting back a smile. "Oh dear. They take after you, do they, Pandora?"

"Luckily, they get their hard heads from their papa," Penny muttered. "Owen didn't suffer so much as a bruise."

Marcus smiled. "You must come see the hoodlums for yourself, Sister Agatha. And you will be the judge of who has the right of it, me or my wife."

"Thank you for the invitation, my lord. I'd like to pay a visit to London soon to meet your family, but with the reconstruction of the Abbey underway, all hands are needed at present. In fact, I'll be heading back tomorrow."

"So soon? No, you must stay," Penny said, looking crestfallen. "We have so much to catch up on—"

"I'm needed back at the Abbey, dear," Agatha said gently but firmly. "I came because your note concerned me. I'm relieved to see that I had nothing to worry about."

"Out of curiosity, what did Penny's note say?" Marcus asked.

Crinkles of humor deepened around Agatha's eyes. "As I recall, her exact words were, *I love my husband too well to let some trollop have him. So I shall have to resort to kidnapping him and bringing him back to our cottage in the Cotswolds where our marriage first began and where I hope we can begin again.*" The lady smiled at Penny, who was blushing furiously. "The word *kidnapping* caught my attention, so I thought it best to come take a look. But clearly I needn't have worried."

"I appreciate your concern for Penny." Sliding a wicked glance at his spouse, he said, "For future reference, you should know that I have given her permission to kidnap me any time the urge comes over her."

"*Marcus*," Penny hissed, her cheeks afire.

Chuckling, he caught her hand and kissed it, saying, "I believe that's my cue to leave you two ladies to your reminiscing." Rising, he bowed to Agatha. "Good evening, ma'am. It was the greatest pleasure to meet you at last."

"The pleasure was mine, my lord."

───────

After Marcus left, Penny said eagerly, "Well, what do you think of him?"

"It hardly matters what I think, my dear. But from what I witnessed this evening,"—Agatha smiled her gentle smile—"he is perfect for you. Everything you said he was."

"Isn't he the best of husbands? I'm the luckiest woman in the world," Penny said happily.

"Yes." Agatha's expression grew contemplative. "And you trust him, my dear?"

"Of course I do. He's forgiven me for being a spy, for my past. And even for lying... um, on our wedding night." Penny's cheeks heated.

"You'll recall that I didn't approve of that particular ploy," Agatha said dryly.

"I know you didn't. At the time, I felt as if I didn't have a choice."

"Dearest, I said it before, and I'll say it again: you underrate your own worth. You always have." Lines deepened on Agatha's brow. "And although I don't wish to speak ill of the dead, I still blame Octavian for the role he played in that."

At the mention of the spymaster, Penny's midsection clenched, but she said, "That's all water under the bridge. Marcus knows the truth now, and I shan't ever lie to him again."

"Does your husband know the entire truth?"

Agatha's soft words and keen glance made Penny's pulse skip. The other didn't say any more—and she didn't have to. They both knew what she was referring to.

"Everything he needs to know," Penny said in a low, firm voice.

Leaning forward, her friend took her hands, which had turned cold despite the warmth of the fire. "You have nothing to be ashamed of. What happened to you—"

"I don't want to talk about it." Penny pulled away.

"Fear is a cage," Agatha persisted. "Truth is the key to setting you free."

"I am free. I have a husband who loves me, a family I adore." She swallowed. "I have everything I need."

"I once told myself that, too." One of Agatha's hands reached upward, her fingers brushing against the silver locket that hung against her grey bodice. "When Harry was taken from me and in such a senseless way, it took me a long time to accept that God has a plan for all of us. Losing Harry destroyed my life as I knew it, yet his death forced me to find another path, one that has since led me to my true calling. I loved Harry with all my heart, and because espionage was his passion, I took it on too, even though I never liked it. I wanted only to help those in need—and that is what I'm doing now. In a fashion that finally allows me peace."

"I'm glad you found that, Agatha," Penny said tremulously. "No one deserves it more."

"My point is that even terrible things—losses and tragedies—might bring a lesson in their wake," the other replied. "Have you considered that perhaps the Spectre's reemergence was no coincidence? That there might have been a reason for him to rear his ugly head when he did? That mayhap it was a sign that the time was ripe for the truth—Your Truth—to emerge?"

Darkness welled, a rising tide that filled Penny with panic. With the fear that this time she wouldn't be able to keep it at bay. That the degradation she'd worked so hard to put behind her would destroy the beauty of her present.

"Please, speak of it no more," she pleaded. "Let's not ruin our first reunion in twelve years."

Agatha regarded her for a long moment then sighed. "You know I only want the best for you, my dear."

"I know." Her voice quivered. "But you have to trust me when I say that things are good. I'm happy. Happier than I deserve to be."

Reaching out a hand, Agatha cupped her cheek. "One day, my dearest..." Their gazes held; her friend's brown eyes were solemn and a little sad. "I hope you'll realize what you truly deserve."

The next morning, Penny said goodbye to Agatha. Neither of them were for long farewells, but that didn't prevent them from clinging to one another and promising to visit soon. Marcus handed Agatha up into the driver's seat of the wagon.

"Please expect a donation for the Abbey. A grateful token for all you've done," he said.

Knowing that he wasn't just referring to Agatha's charitable works, Penny felt a burgeoning of all she felt for him—for his goodness and honor.

I love him so much. The thought ought to have been joyous; for some reason, it was tinged with desperation. *All will be well*, she told herself. It was just that the conversation with Agatha had dug up ghosts; soon they would settle again—she would shut them out, make them go away as she'd always done.

"Thank you, my lord," Agatha was saying serenely. "I have no gift in return, but, if I may, I'd like to offer a small blessing."

Marcus inclined his head, his arm circling Penny's waist.

"May the both of you know the bounty which you've been given and surrender your trust,"—her brown eyes fixed on Penny —"in the Good Lord's grace."

Agatha's words lingered after her departure, spurring in Penny a keen urgency to make the most of every moment she had with Marcus. He seemed to share this sentiment; Agatha's wagon had barely reached the snowy woods when he swung Penny into his arms and carried her back into the cottage, smothering her giggles with his kiss.

So the day went.

That night, sated and content, Penny fell asleep in Marcus' arms, surrounded by his warm and solid presence.

She woke up screaming.

"Penny, love. I'm here. You're safe."

The voice wasn't coming from the alley. From the darkness holding her down, choking her. Her lungs strained to pull in air. Light flared, blinding her.

The floating spots faded to her husband.

It's Marcus. It's Marcus. Her disoriented mind clung to those words, the details of him, the way a drowning person does to driftwood.

The worried lines on his face, blue eyes bright with concern. His chest was bare, shadows dancing over rippling muscle. He was sitting next to her, bedclothes tangled around his lean waist.

The bedchamber. The cottage at the Cotswolds.

He reached a hand to her, and she couldn't stop the flinch.

Surprise flitted across his features. "You've had a nightmare, darling. A bad one. But you're safe." His voice was deep and soothing, the one he used with the boys when they were hurt and in need of comfort. "You're here with me."

"Yes." Her insides were coiled so tightly that she could hardly get the word out.

He reached a hand out again, this time slowly, and she

managed to hold still as his palm cupped her cheek. Wetness slid against his callused skin. His eyes held hers.

"Do you want to talk about it?" he said.

"It... it's nothing. Just a dream. As you said."

"You're shivering all over, darling. Come here."

She allowed herself to be gathered against his chest. Her skin was chilled, clammy, and she soaked in his warmth as he pulled the blankets over them both. Cuddled against him, trembling, she could hear his steady, strong heartbeat, and it rooted her in the present. She rubbed her cheek against his hard chest, the wiry scratch of hair another needed reminder that this was real. That she was here. Not there.

I'm with Marcus. I'm safe.

"After Waterloo, I used to have dreams." His voice rumbled beneath her ear. Easy and conversational. Lulling. "Bad ones. Of battle. Remember the time I woke you during our wedding trip?"

She'd forgotten, but the memory came back.

"Here, in this bed," she managed.

"Yes. I woke up terrified. Of the dream, but mostly of scaring you. Of the fact that my bride of five days might think me a lunatic."

"I didn't think that."

"No, you didn't." He stroked her hair, his touch as warm and reassuring as his voice. "What you did was hold me and make me talk about it. You listened and never judged. You did that every time I had a nightmare, and eventually, I stopped having them."

Her pulse sped up; she knew where this was headed.

"Trust me to do the same for you, love," he said.

"I... I'm scared."

"Of the dream?"

"Yes. But more so..."—her voice cracked against the hard core of it—"of what you'll think. Of me."

"Nothing can change that. You're my love, my Penny, and you'll always be."

"I almost lost you. I don't want to risk that again—"

"Darling, you couldn't lose me in Covent Garden on market day."

That made her lift her head. "That's not true. If I hadn't kidnapped you, you might be with Cora Ashley. Our marriage would still be in danger—"

"Hell, Penny, is that what you think?" His eyes radiated genuine disbelief. "I would never go to Cora Ashley—or any other woman for that matter. You're the only one for me. I've told you that."

He had, in fact. Repeatedly.

At the time, she'd known his assurances were genuine, and she'd believed them... hadn't she? Confusion and shame rippled through her. *Why is it so hard for me to believe?*

He sat them both up against the pillows so that they were facing each other. Holding her hands in his, he said, "I acted like a bastard because I was hurt. That doesn't excuse how I treated you, and you have my word that I'll do my utmost not to lash out at you like that again. But you must know this: even if my faith in our marriage suffered a brief crisis, my love for you never faltered."

"How could it not?" she blurted. "I hid the fact that I was a spy. That I... I wasn't a virgin."

Instinct made her brace herself. She watched his expression, waiting for it to harden.

It didn't.

Instead, his gaze unwavering, he said, "I slept with over a dozen women before I met you, Penny. Thirteen, to be exact. Did you know that?"

She didn't. "No."

"Are you going to hold it against me?"

"Of course not."

"Did you sleep with anyone after we met on the Pilkingtons' balcony?"

"No," she said cautiously.

"What about after our very first meeting—Christmas at the camp?"

She shook her head.

"Then I don't care," he said firmly. "I don't care what you did before me. Because from the moment we met, you've been mine, Penny. I was just too stupid and angry to realize it when you first told me of your past."

"I shouldn't have lied to you," she said in a small voice.

"So don't do it now." His eyes were soft, inviting. "If we've learned anything from all of this, it's that we can trust our love to survive mistakes. Your lies, my foolish behavior. Our love can get us through anything."

"I was raped." The words burst from her.

In the silence that followed, her heart thundered in her ears, wings of panic beating in her breast. She saw the flames explode in Marcus' eyes, and every fiber of her braced for the worst.

"Penny. My God." He cupped her jaw. His hands shook, yet he touched her with such care and tenderness that her throat thickened. "When?"

"Around the time I met Octavian."

She saw raw pain slice across her husband's features. His eyes closed briefly. When his lashes lifted, she saw the fire had been banked in those vibrant depths. His jaw quivered, betraying the sheer strength he was employing to keep his emotions in check. And he was doing it for her.

So she gave him more. "I was out late selling flowers. A man said he wanted to buy some but had forgotten his coin purse at his lodgings. He said if I followed him he'd take the rest of the lot in my basket. I knew better, but I was tired, and that day I hadn't sold or stolen enough to buy the night's supper. So I went with him."

Marcus said nothing, listening, his silence more reassuring than any words.

Strangely enough, talking about this didn't feel as bad as she'd feared it would. As she gave voice to the details, they seemed... muted somehow. Like something she was watching happen in the distance. Or through a pane of frosted glass.

"He forced me into an alleyway. Left me there afterward." Her throat convulsed. "That's how Octavian found me."

Marcus' chest surged, his hands holding firmly onto hers. "God, Penny." His words were rough with emotion, and to her shock, she saw that his eyes were wet. "You must have been frightened out of your wits."

"I was, at first. But Octavian said something to me that took away the fear. He bundled me in his cloak and said, *If it's justice you want, come with me. I vow not to hurt you and to give you the weapons to avenge your honor.*"

"You were a girl," her husband said, his voice turning low and dangerous, "and a hurt and vulnerable one at that. What the hell was he thinking?"

"He'd seen me in action in Covent Garden. I'd caught his eye when he was there tracking down a Frenchman named Vincent Barone, an enemy agent notorious for his cruelty and ruthlessness, his love of inflicting pain." Her heart thumping, she forced herself to go on. "As Fate would have it, Octavian's enemy and mine turned out to be the same. Thus, I dedicated myself to the training he offered: the art of disguise, combat, coding—I learned everything that I could."

In truth, she'd soaked it up like a thirsty sponge. The need for revenge had displaced helplessness, given her a sense of power. Recalling how Octavian's approval of her progress had meant the world to her, she felt that old twinge of bitterness. But it was just a twinge, tempered now by an acceptance of who she'd been: a young girl in need of a parent, some older, wiser figure. It happened that the man she'd chosen for that role valued ambition more than anything else, including those who'd worked for him.

Still, in some ways, she owed Octavian her life.

"Three years later, in a brothel in Dieppe, I had the opportunity to mete out my justice," she went on. "Barone didn't recognize me in my disguise, drank the wine I served him. And when he lay there, dying, I told him exactly who I was and why his next breath would be his last. I walked out of there knowing I wasn't powerless anymore."

Even as the words spilled from her like water from a dam, anxiety frothed inside her. God, she sounded so... ruthless. Aggressive and cold-blooded, like no lady would ever sound. Was Marcus shocked? Had she succeeded in disgusting him at last?

"The bastard deserved to die." Marcus' tone was savage. "My only regret about his death is that I cannot kill him all over again. I'd like to tear the bugger from limb to limb, rip his bloody heart out."

Her heart thudding, she saw the primal intent in Marcus' eyes, his fierce expression. It was the look of a man who meant what he'd said: he would kill for her. He would avenge the wrong that had been done to his woman. Such brutal justice might offend the sensibilities of a well-bred lady, but to Penny it was a revelation.

Finally she *felt* the truth of what he'd told her time and again. He loved her. Loved *her.* No matter what and with a ferocity that satisfied her deepest longings.

He loved her the way she loved him.

Certainty flooded her, along with a relief so great that she felt her soul let out a sigh. It made it easy to let go of the rest. To cleanse herself of the past once and for all.

"The other two men I was with were part of missions. Chenet and Martin—they were nothing but means to an end. Octavian had taught me to use every weapon available to me, including my physical charms. At the time, I thought it was a form of power. I wasn't going to be anyone's victim again; I was going to use *them.* I thought that, in using my body, *I* was in control. Flora tried to dissuade me from that dark path, told me I was trading one devil for another. She said I deserved far better."

"I'm adding a full bloody wing to Flora's Abbey."

Marcus' grim and unexpected humor startled a gurgled laugh from her throat. She hadn't ever imagined that she could feel lightness while talking about her past; it was yet another gift he'd given her.

Now it was her turn to take his face in her hands. His bristly jaw was quivering with what he was feeling for her, but his eyes burned with love.

"Then I met you that Christmas," she said softly, "and you made me recognize the truth of Flora's words. That I did deserve better. That I would do anything to have your love, the love of a good man."

"By God, you have it. I love you, Penny. More than anything in the world."

His kiss simmered with intensity. An answering fire leapt within her, billowed by a pure freedom that she'd never known before. Love and lust combusted, blasting through her. But when she parted her lips to deepen their connection, he drew back.

"Are you certain you want this now, love?" His voice was strained, his gaze searching. "You've gone through a lot tonight. I could just hold you—"

"Make love to me, Marcus." Her hands speared through his hair. "I need this. I need *you*."

His eyes blazed into hers. "Whatever you need, you'll have it."

Then he was kissing her, truly kissing her, giving her the passion she craved, the bright flame of his love melting away her shadows. He shoved away the sheets, sat up against the pillows and rolled her on top of him. He continued kissing her until she was panting, squirming, delirious with desire. The thick iron bar of his cock throbbed against her thigh, the temptation almost too much to bear.

"I want you," she whispered.

His nostrils flared, his pupils darkening. "Take me then. Whatever you want, Penny, it's yours."

Her heartbeat kicked up a notch. She knew why he was giving her the power, and she loved him all the more for it... but, blooming hell, how was she to *choose* what she wanted? It was like being given carte blanche at a sweets shop. She wanted her delicious husband in every way she could have him.

She began by kissing his jaw, the strong column of his neck. His warm masculine scent curled in her nostrils as she moved down to his upper torso, running her fingers over the lean slabs of muscle, loving the virile rasp of his chest hair. Bending down, she kissed his coppery nipples, teasing the flat discs with her tongue, smiling when she heard the hitch in his breath.

She trailed kisses over his ribs, the ridges of his abdomen flexing beneath her lips. Nudging his muscular thighs apart, she made room for herself there, the way a cat does in a sunny spot. As she eyed her lord's masculine bounty, she did feel rather like a feline presented with a dish of the richest, tastiest cream.

"Keep looking at me like that, love," he said, humor threading through his deep voice, "and it'll be over before you know it."

She curled her fingers around his huge shaft, so erect and hard that she had to pry it gently away from his stomach. "From first-hand experience, I can vouch for your staying power, Lord Blackwood."

"If those hands of yours continue what they're doing, Lady Blackwood,"—his eyes grew hooded as she ran her fist from thick root to fat, glistening tip—"you may be in for a surprise."

"You don't like my hands?" She made a moue.

"Do I look as though I don't like your hands?" he said dryly.

A droplet of his essence formed on his cockhead, punctuating his point. The pearly bead invited her to lean forward and lick it off. So she did. The clean, salty taste of him tingled on her tongue.

"*Christ*, woman."

His voice sounded strangled, likely because she was in the process of trying to swallow his entire shaft. She loved taking him this way, his proud heat filling her, his hips bucking when he hit the back of her throat. She bobbed her head on his cock, her hands cupping and rubbing his heavy stones the way she knew he liked, and his hands clenched in her hair.

Not guiding or controlling her. Just holding on as she took what she wanted.

It made her want more.

She slid her mouth upward, releasing him with a moist *pop*. Propped up against the pillows, he watched her, loving lust in his blue eyes. Holding his gaze, she clambered astride him, reaching down to align their bodies. She sank down on his meaty pole, impaling herself in a swift stroke, crying out with the pleasure of it.

"Bloody hell, I love being inside you." His voice was a sensual rasp. "Your pussy is so wet and hot and greedy for my cock, isn't it?"

"Yes." She gasped as his rod jerked inside her.

"Then take what you want. Fuck me, Penny."

She needed no further urging. Balancing a hand on his shoulder, she rocked her hips, sliding up and then slamming all the way down. He growled, and she did it again, pleasure welling at her very center. It spread outward, sweetness singing through her limbs as she rode her husband's cock, and he let her dictate the pace. Gave her anything she wanted. Made her feel loved and powerful, free to be who she was.

With exhilarating abandon, she gyrated on his shaft and cupped her breasts.

"Kiss me, Marcus," she invited.

His eyes flared, and he wasted no time in taking what she offered. The hot suck of his mouth shot straight to her pussy, which clenched around his wide girth, making them both groan. He tongued her nipples as she rode him faster and faster, needful of the finish just in the distance. She was so close, her muscles tautening, her insides trembling for want of relief, but she couldn't quite get there.

His thumb slid to where they were joined, right where she needed it.

"Blooming hell," she gasped.

Her head flung back as she shot over the precipice, propelled into toe-curling, mind-melting bliss.

The next instant, she was on her back. Marcus was over her. His face dark with passion, he drove into her. The hard, pounding strokes fueled her rippling climax. The pleasure went on and on, and she didn't know if she came again or if her orgasm simply didn't stop. She hung on, riding the waves of it, and then his big body shuddered and he shouted out her name. His heat flooded her, warming her very core.

He collapsed onto the bed, rolled her atop him, keeping their bodies joined. He stroked her hair as she cuddled against him, her cheek pressed to his chest. Lulled by his strong and steady heart, his whispers of love, she drifted into a contented sleep.

❧ 24 ❧

1827

Marcus entered his wife's bedchamber and smiled at the gorgeous picture she made. Sitting at her vanity, she was dressed in a vibrant fuchsia gown that emphasized her tempting figure. Her maid Jenny stood by her side, an open jewelry chest before them.

The maid tied a pearl choker around Penny's neck, muttering, "No, that's not quite right either, is it, milady?"

Apparently, he'd come just in time. He came forward.

"Marcus... you look splendid," Penny said, her eyes meeting his in the mirror.

He loved the breathy quality to her voice when she said that. When she looked at him this way as if, to her, he were the only man on earth, and she saw no one else. It made him feel powerful and bloody lucky... and he had to stop thinking about how lucky he was or he would ruin the smoothly pressed front of his trousers with a raging cockstand.

Pausing at Penny's side, he bent and kissed her cheek, breathing in the subtle allure of jasmine and neroli.

"I can take it from here," he told the maid.

Jenny, being a longtime retainer, had a knowing twinkle in her eyes. Placing the pearls back into the jewelry chest, she closed its lid and, with a quick curtsy, scurried off.

Marcus removed the flat velvet box from his pocket and handed it to Penny.

"Our tenth anniversary isn't until next week," she said, smiling at him.

"I know. But since our Summer Soiree is about to begin and, knowing you, the house will be Bedlam and run over with eager guests,"—he winked to let her know he was teasing her—"I thought you might like to debut this tonight."

"You're the best of husbands," she said, her voice tremulous.

He loved that she thought that—and she hadn't yet seen her present.

"Open it, darling," he said.

She did, and the gasp that left her lips was worth every penny he'd spent on the extravagant piece of jewelry.

"Marcus... it's extraordinary," she breathed. "I've never seen anything this beautiful."

"I have," he murmured. "Let me help you put it on."

He lifted the necklace and set it against his marchioness' satiny skin. He smiled in satisfaction at the reflection. The collar of large, deep red rubies connected by strands of flawless diamonds suited his Penny perfectly.

His eyes met hers in the mirror.

"For my wife," he said huskily, "whose price is above rubies."

Penny's eyes shimmered. "It's too much. But I love it. I love *you.*"

"As I love you, my darling."

She came to her feet and threw her arms around his neck with a ferocity that might have knocked over a lesser man. He merely wrapped his arms around her waist.

"I don't deserve you, Marcus. I don't," she said, her voice muffled. "But I'll make you proud, I swear it."

Puzzled, he set her back, looked into her tear-bright eyes. "You're everything I've ever wanted, Penny. I couldn't be prouder to be your husband. If you don't know that, then *I'm* doing something wrong."

"I do... I do know it." She bit her lip. "It's just that I... oh, I'm overwhelmed. Thank you, Marcus. For the necklace. For loving me."

"You're welcome," he said softly, "though no thanks are necessary."

She expelled a breath, smoothed her skirts. Nabbing a handkerchief from the vanity, she dabbed at her eyes. "Heavens, I must look a fright. And with guests coming at any moment, too."

"You are the most beautiful woman I've ever seen," he said solemnly.

"Don't—you're going to make me cry again."

"All right. I'll save my praise for after the party."

"That you can do." In one of her lightning quick changes, she flashed a sultry smile that made his blood run hotter. "At that time, I'll give you your proper thanks, too."

"We have a deal." He offered her his arm. "Ready to greet the mob, Lady Blackwood?"

"Of course, Lord Blackwood."

They went down to welcome their guests.

25

DECEMBER 1829

The smashing of China greeted Penny as she entered the foyer, Marcus at her side.

"Ethan made me do it!" Owen immediately jabbed a finger at his brother.

"I did not. You're just a clumsy oaf," Ethan shot back.

"I'm not an oaf!" Owen's face turned red. "If you hadn't pushed me when we were going round the corner, I wouldn't have bumped the table, and the vase wouldn't have fallen. It's *your* fault."

"I saw everything," Jamie volunteered. "Owen was running too fast, *and* Ethan pushed him. Therefore, it was both their faults."

"Tattletale," Ethan muttered.

"*Boys*." The dowager's cane rapped the marble floor. She came up slowly behind the squabbling trio, her eyes narrowed above the froth of black lace that covered her to her chin. "That's quite enough out of you. Your parents have only just arrived home, and there you are carrying on like residents of Bedlam."

Before the dowager could scold them some more, Penny intervened. Opening her arms, she said, "Come say hello, my darlings."

They rushed forward. She hugged them each in turn, inhaling their little boy smells and kissing their sweet, squirmy cheeks. Lord, how she'd missed them.

Jamie escaped to his father. "I learned a theorem by Pythagorus this week, Papa," he said, man-to-man. "I can derive a proof from it."

Marcus clapped a hand on their eldest's shoulder. "That's quite an accomplishment, son."

"I've been reading all about the Romans." Ethan bounded over. "I know the Emperors by heart, beginning with Augustus."

"Well done, Ethan. We'll hear a recitation before supper," Marcus said.

Owen approached his father last. He crooked his finger, and Marcus obligingly bent down so that their youngest could whisper something in his ear. When he straightened, his lips were curved.

"That's quite an accomplishment, lad," he said.

Owen beamed with relief. "You think so, Papa?"

Marcus placed a big hand atop Owen's dark mop. "Absolutely."

"What did you tell Papa that you did?" Ethan said.

"It's between me and Papa." Owen lifted his chin. "And I won't tell you because you'll just make fun."

"Only if it's something stupid," Ethan retorted.

"I'm not stupid!"

"Boys." Marcus' firm tone cut the squabble short. "Let us remove to the drawing room where you may each fill me in on the rest of your week."

"Yes, Papa," the three chorused as one.

Marcus winked at Penny, stopped to kiss her lightly on the mouth, and led the way out. Falling obediently in line, the boys trooped after their father.

"I don't know how he does that," Penny mused aloud.

Her mama-in-law snorted. "He does that by not coddling them and spoiling them rotten."

Although tempted to argue, Penny decided to take the higher road. The fact that she was fairly floating on happiness made it easier to bite her tongue.

"It was kind of you to look after the boys in our absence. Thank you," she said politely.

"Given the perilous state of your marriage, I had no choice. So let us dispense with the formalities—I'm far too old for such nonsense." The dowager waved an impatient hand. "What I want to know is whether you've succeeded in winning my son back from that licentious tart Cora Ashley."

Penny stared at the older lady. "How... how did you know about Lady Ashley?"

"The whole Town's abuzz over it. Some wag saw you running from your own ball as if the devil himself were after you. Someone else saw my Marcus emerging from a balcony and that despicable Lady Ashley came out of the same said balcony not two minutes later." The dowager's knuckles whitened on the jeweled knob of her cane. "Everyone's put two and two together and come up with four. I knew about the gossip even before you came to me for help, but since you looked as lost as a babe in the woods, I decided you didn't need to trip over rumors whilst you were attempting to find your path. I assumed that your little *business trip* with Marcus was an attempt to win my son back." Her mama-in-law arched a brow. "Since the two of you appear to be lovebirds once again, your plan succeeded, did it not?"

Penny didn't know whether to feel annoyed or grateful. "First of all, I didn't have to win Marcus back from anyone," she retorted. "Especially not the likes of Cora Ashley. He loves me and only me."

"I know that. I raised my son to be a good and loyal man, and he would never betray the vows he made to his wife. Even so, one tempts Fate by leaving the doors open wide and unlocked for any thief to march through." The dowager aimed a stern look at her. "You really must guard your valuables better in the future, my dear."

"I'll keep that in mind," Penny said through her teeth.

"Well, then, that's settled." Her mama-in-law gave her an imperious look. "There's only one more thing to attend to."

"And that is?"

"Suppressing the scandal, of course. We can't have the world thinking anything's amiss between the Blackwoods." The dowager's eyes narrowed. "I never liked that Cora Ashley. Always said she was too common by far."

Penny could actually feel the divots in her tongue, formed by the many times she'd had to bite it during this conversation. But... she would let bygones be bygones.

"'Tis easier to stop the flow of the Thames than gossip once it's started," she stated.

Her mama-in-law harrumphed. "Shows how much you know, my girl. Well, take it from one who has been around the *ton* several decades longer than you: there's a solution for everything. It is merely a matter of committing one's mind to the problem."

"I'm dying to hear what you've come up with," Penny said.

"You shan't have to expire, my dear." The dowager gave her a sardonic look. "I shall simply tell you."

"Your mama has bats in her belfry," Penny announced.

As this was not the first time his wife had made such a statement during the years of their marriage and likely not the last, Marcus said mildly, "Oh?"

Penny set her brush down on the vanity with a click and stalked over to where he was lounging on the bed. He noted with interest that she didn't appear to be wearing anything beneath her emerald satin robe.

She braced her hands on her hips. "Apparently the Ashleys are giving a Christmas Ball, and your mother thinks we ought to go."

"Oh?" He was right—she wasn't wearing anything. He could see her tight, hard nipples poking against the delicate fabric. He felt himself getting hard under his own dressing gown.

"*Oh*—is that all you have to say?"

Other possibilities leapt into his mind. *Come closer so I can suckle your breasts. Would you prefer to ride me tonight, or shall we try another position?* He tried to focus on his wife's words. "What is the problem, precisely?"

"The problem, *Marcus*,"—never a good thing when she said his name in that tone—"is that I have no intention of gracing that trollop's house with my presence."

Understanding pierced his playful mood. With remorse, he said quietly, "I acted like a fool, but you do know that I have no interest whatsoever in Cora Ashley, don't you, love?"

"Of course I know that." The indignant fire in Penny's eyes eased the knot in his chest. Pacing back and forth alongside the bed, she said, "That's not the point."

"Then what is?"

"No bitch in heat is going to wriggle her rump at you and try to take what is mine."

He choked back a laugh. "Er, pardon me?"

"You heard me. She's like a farmyard beast after you to rut her." Penny narrowed her eyes at him. "Are you laughing at me?"

He was trying not to. Ever since the revelations at the cottage, Penny seemed freer, more confident, more... herself. Previously hidden facets of her caught the light, sparkling brilliantly. Although he didn't want his wife to suffer unnecessarily, he couldn't help but find her feminine jealousy rather delightful— especially since it made her breasts surge against her neckline and her eyes blaze with violet flames. An intriguing image flitted through his head, one evoked by Penny's discussion of farmyard mating rituals.

As a result, he was no longer getting hard—he was fully there.

"No," he said contritely. "But your description was rather... colorful."

Penny sniffed. "It's the truth."

"Be that as it may, you may want to consider Mama's advice."

"What?" his wife said in outrage.

"You and I both know nothing happened, but if we don't go to the Ashleys' party, it will only fuel the gossip. The best way to deal with this is head on. We put in an appearance, and we leave. Once everyone sees that there's no friction between us and the Ashleys and thus no cause for drama, the rumors will die. End of story."

He could see that his reasoning hit home... even if she didn't like it. Huffing out a breath, she said, "You're assuming a lot."

He raised a brow. "In what regard?"

"In the regard that I'll be able to hold myself back from using my garotte on bloody Cora Ashley," Penny groused. "We'll see about friction then."

Chuckling, he snagged her hand and pulled her onto the bed so that she was sprawled atop him. "Don't pack your garotte in your reticule that night," he advised, "and you'll do fine."

"Oh, all right." Just as it always did, her storm passed. The fire in her eyes was replaced by a different sort altogether. A wicked, sensual spark that made his blood run hot. "Darling, do you have something in your pocket," she purred, "or are you just *very* happy to see me?"

"All that talk of rutting may have put ideas in my mind," he murmured, running his hands through the wild raven silk of her hair.

"Oh? Any ideas you'd care to share?"

"Why don't I show you instead?" he said.

Crushing her mouth to his, he set about doing just that.

26

It was small of her, Penny knew, but as she and Marcus waited in the long receiving line, she took in the ballroom with a touch of smugness. Cora Ashley's blood might be bluer than Penny's, but the former wouldn't know taste if it knocked her over and dragged her down the street. Penny could tell the countess had poured a small fortune into the night's endeavor and, with all that blunt, managed to create an ambience that was both overblown and unwelcoming.

One couldn't walk two steps without a suspended sprig of mistletoe smacking one in the forehead. The orchestra was three times as large as it needed to be, its volume so deafening that guests were shouting at each other to be heard. The buffet table was piled high with fussy, greasy bits that appealed to neither eye nor stomach. Yet in Penny's opinion, out of all of this, it was the champagne fountain that truly took the cake.

Even from a distance, she could see the towering gold monstrosity. It stood some twelve feet high, frothing forth champagne tinted what (she guessed) was supposed to be a jolly, seasonal shade, but there was no denying what it actually looked like: blood. To Penny, the thing was as grotesque as it was impractical. Every now and again, a cry erupted from some unsuspecting guest when the fountain belched and doused them with a gory spray of red.

As Penny and Marcus approached their hostess in the receiving line, however, her eyes narrowed. Whatever one could say about Cora Ashley's party throwing skills, she clearly had a masterful eye when it came to fashion. The demure, ruffled white creation looked simple but must have cost a pretty penny, the skirts floating elegantly around her slender figure. With her pale blond hair and blue eyes, she looked every inch an angel.

In comparison, Penny had chosen a bold gown of crimson velvet that clung lovingly to her curves. Her ruby necklace was her main accessory, and she wore it with pride as she faced her nemesis.

"How good of you both to come," Cora said in a breathy voice, her eyes fixed on Marcus.

"Thank you, my lady. Lord Ashley." Marcus inclined his head politely at their host and hostess, his face expressionless. "My wife didn't want to miss it."

The Earl of Ashley, a short, balding fellow who smelled as if he'd bathed in brandy, gave them an indifferent greeting and continued flirting with a young matron. His bloodshot eyes glued to her low-cut décolletage, he waddled off with her, abandoning his receiving duties altogether.

"Heavens!" Cora gave a little shriek.

The pressure in Penny's veins shot up as the blonde threw herself against Marcus' chest.

"A spider," Cora gasped. "It just ran over my slipper."

With clear distaste, Marcus set her aside. "I don't see a spider."

"If there's an insect lurking about," Penny said, her jaw clenching, "I'll gladly squash it."

Patting her skirts into place, Cora recovered herself and aimed a saccharine smile at Penny. "Oh, but I wouldn't want you to ruin your slipper, my dear Lady Blackwood. Or your striking ensemble. May I mention how very festive you look?" The subtle emphasis on the word *festive* implied a far less flattering adjective. "I couldn't pull off such a gown, and I daresay not many ladies could."

"Well, I couldn't pull off yours," Penny said, just as sweetly. "White is such a virtuous shade. I fear it makes one's true colors shine through."

Splotches formed on Cora's cheeks.

Marcus' arm tightened around Penny's waist. "Come, darling, let's not hold up the line. I'll get you some champagne."

He dragged her away.

"I wasn't finished," Penny said under her breath.

"You're finished."

"She had the *gall* to insult my dress—you heard that, didn't you?"

"I heard it."

"And there was no bleeding spider," Penny fumed.

"I know." His jaw tautened, and he turned a brooding gaze to her. "I'm sorry I didn't realize what her true character was before. And even sorrier to put you through this."

She tipped her head to one side. Grinned as the realization hit her. "Are you admitting that you were wrong about Cora Ashley and I was right?"

"Yes." He sounded disgruntled.

"Well, then. Maybe coming tonight was worth it after all."

A reluctant smile tugged on his lips. "You're incorrigible, do you know that?"

"You love it about me," she said confidently.

"Since I love everything about you, you have the right of it yet again. On that note, since we are here for the duration, would you care to dance?"

"I would." She gave him a cheeky look. "And while we waltz,

you may continue to whisper sweet nothings in my ear of how I'm *always* right."

He laughed. "Anything you want, my Penny. Anything you want."

Penny reflected that the ball wasn't half as bad as she'd thought it would be. Cora Ashley had been unmasked at last. Penny got to waltz with Marcus twice, and if the passionate way he'd whirled her across the dance floor didn't quell the rumors of their estrangement, then Society could go hang itself. Finally, the Kent ladies had showed up at the ball, and Penny was now enjoying a splendid chat with them.

All in all, it was turning out to be a fine evening. She snuck a glance at Marcus; he was standing across the ballroom, conversing with an inarguably masculine and virile group that included Viscount Carlisle and some other cronies. Call her biased, but she had no eyes for anyone but her husband. God, but she loved Marcus in formal evening wear. She looked forward to tearing it off him after the party, piece by tailored piece.

"You look like the cat that got the canary. Or, in this case, her husband."

She returned her attention back to her circle, which included Emma, Thea, and Marianne Kent. The latter was giving her a knowing smile.

Penny didn't bother to hide her satisfaction. "Yes."

"You seem like newlyweds. It's very romantic," Thea said with a sigh.

"Thea would know," Emma put in. "Since she is, in fact, an actual newlywed."

"Didn't you just return from dancing with Strathaven... again?" Thea raised her fair brows.

A grin tucked into the duchess' cheeks. "Better to dance than argue, I always say. I think His Grace spins me extra quickly so that I lose my breath and he can get the last word in."

"Where are your husbands, by the by?" Penny asked.

She was used to seeing the rather possessive gentlemen keeping a close watch on their ladies. Then again, she thought with a thrum of pleasure, Marcus was no different. He caught her eye just then and gave her a wink.

"They've been assigned to Violet duty, and they're taking shifts," Emma said matter-of-factly. "We figured that, between the three men, they might manage to keep Vi out of hot water."

"Speaking of hot, is it just me, or is it positively sweltering in here?" Marianne said, waving her feathered fan. "Does Lady Ashley understand nothing of ventilation? I've been in Roman baths less steamy than this ballroom."

Obligingly, a liveried footman approached with a tray in hand. "Refreshments, miladies?"

"Yes, please," Thea said.

He handed them each a frosted flute in turn, saving the last for Penny. Her fingers curling around the stem, she drank some of the peach-colored beverage. It was pleasantly cold and sweet, but it had an undernote that she couldn't place.

"What's in the punch?" Penny said. "I don't recognize the flavor."

"It's a blend of spices, I think." In line with her practical nature, Emma had a flare for cookery—unusual for a duchess. "I taste ginger, cinnamon, nutmeg... and a hint of anise, too." She wrinkled her nose. "Bit much, if you ask me."

"I don't care what's in it as long as it's cold," Marianne said.

Penny couldn't agree more. "Bottoms up," she said and finished her glass.

Ten minutes later, she excused herself from the group to use the retiring room. Her stomach felt queasy—probably the heat and the fatty, nasty hors d'oeuvres she ought to have avoided altogether. She exited the ballroom, and, as she made her way down the empty corridor, she stumbled, barely catching herself against the wall. She shook her head, which was suddenly... woozy.

What's the matter with me?

Another wave of dizziness swamped her, and she tripped again.

Someone gripped her arm, preventing her fall.

Her head flopped back. The face blurred in and out of focus before she recognized it.

The footman.

"Help me," she managed.

"Come this way, my lady. I have a place for you to rest."

Blooming hell... the punch...

That was her last thought before darkness closed in.

❧ 27 ❧

"Have you seen my wife?" Marcus asked the trio of Kent ladies.

"About a quarter hour ago, I think," Mrs. Kent said. "She was headed off to the retiring room, but she ought to be back by now."

Tremont arrived and handed his marchioness a glass of lemonade.

"Did you see Lady Blackwood at the buffet tables by any chance?" the latter asked.

"No, princess," Tremont said. "Why?"

"Lord Blackwood is looking for her. She's missing."

"Who's missing, Thea?" This came from Ambrose Kent, who approached his wife and settled an arm around her waist.

"My wife," Marcus said. "None of you have seen her recently?"

Everyone shook their heads.

His nape prickled. He knew his Penny. At social events, they didn't live in each other's pockets, but they did check in with one another. Regularly. It was unlike her to absent herself for so long without telling him where she was going.

"I'm going to look for her," he said.

"For who?" The Duke of Strathaven sauntered over.

"His wife," the duchess said. Her clear brown eyes widened as she took in the newly arrived gentlemen. "One moment. Why are all three of you here... where's Violet?"

"I thought you had her," Strathaven said to Kent.

Kent turned to Tremont. "I thought you did."

"Hell," Tremont said succinctly.

Marcus didn't stay for the rest. He strode out of the ballroom to look for his wife. He was in the hallway heading toward the foyer when a breathy voice called out from behind him. "Blackwood?"

Devil take it.

Turning, he acknowledged curtly, "Lady Ashley."

"You're not leaving already?"

Her voice had a tremulous quiver. In truth, it always had. He didn't know how he'd missed how annoying it was until now.

"I'm looking for my wife," he said. "Have you seen her?"

The countess' lips trembled. She clasped her hands over her chest, her fingers twisting together. "I... I may have."

Relief filled him. "Where?"

"Marcus, please, can't we talk a moment?"

His shoulders stiffened at her overly familiar use of his name.

Her eyes shimmered. "You saw how Ashley was. He doesn't care about me at all. I'm so alone."

Bloody hell.

"That is something to discuss with your husband, my lady," Marcus said coldly.

"But I want to talk to you. Please, Marcus, if we could just go somewhere private—"

"I would not dishonor my wife in such a way," he said in cutting accents. "If you need someone to talk to, find a friend. Now where did you see Penny?"

"Penny." Lady Ashley's mouth formed a thin line. "She's all you care about?"

Finally, the woman was catching on.

"Yes," he affirmed. "She is."

"She's not good enough for you, you know. She never was, even though she stole you from me." Before he could fully digest her vain assumption that he'd ever been hers in the first place, she went on, "You don't have to hide your pain with me, Marcus. I know something's amiss in your marriage, and I'm here to—"

"Because this is your party, I will overlook your insult to my wife this one time. Do it again," he said in glacial tones, "and I won't be so forgiving. Now for the last bloody time, have you seen Penny?"

Lady Ashley's demure mien slipped, and he had a glimpse of something hard and oddly menacing beneath. "In that case, I do believe I saw her go upstairs," she said in a brittle voice. "She was headed for the private gallery."

"Why the hell would she go there?" he said.

"I haven't the faintest. Typically I close that part of the house to guests, but sometimes they take advantage,"—she let out a tinny, tinkling laugh—"of my hospitality."

"Which way?" he said shortly.

"I'll show you."

He had no desire to be in his hostess' company, but if she got him to Penny quicker, then so be it.

"Lead the way," he said.

Penny blinked groggily. Blurred colors and shapes bobbed across her vision. She tried to sit up, but dizziness made her slump backward, her head hitting something hard and strangely warm.

"There, now," a male voice said. "Just lie there and relax. This'll be over soon."

What will be over...? Who is that... What the... blooming hell...?

Her eyelids felt as heavy as lead, but she forced them open. Held them that way until the room settled. A gallery... door at the far end. Gilt-framed portraits that she didn't recognize. She was in the middle of the room... reclined? With dawning horror, she registered the hairy arm around her corseted waist and farther down, her bared legs, cherry silk garters cinched around her thighs and white stockings on her legs. Her velvet dress was slung over the end of the couch.

Buffle-headed and panicked, she started to struggle, but the arm kept her trapped.

A second later, the door opened.

"I do believe I saw her go in here... *oh dear.*"

Penny's heart stopped as she saw Marcus standing there, Cora Ashley clinging to his arm.

"I think we've interrupted a rendezvous," Cora said *sotto voce.*

"Marcus," Penny said hoarsely.

The reality of her situation blazed through her, and despite her woozy state, she renewed her struggle. This time, the arm let her go, and she stumbled to her feet, her bare knee bumping painfully against the coffee table. She stared in shock at the man who'd been keeping her captive on the couch: the footman, his hair disorderly, chest bare, the fall of his trousers hanging open.

He looked like a lover caught in the act of a sexual escapade.

And she looked no better.

The situation was damning; her history made it more so.

Her gaze flew to Marcus, and the fury and disgust on his face made her throat close. Her stomach churned sickly. She couldn't get words out, incoherent pleas dashing against her skull like waves against a rocky shore.

You must believe me... it's not how it looks... no, no, no...

"Come, Blackwood, let's leave them. It's as I said." Cora Ashley placed a hand on Marcus' sleeve, her smile victorious. "She's not worth the scandal to your name."

Marcus shoved her off. The next instant, he was prowling over to Penny. Yanking off his jacket, he placed it gently on her shoulders.

He cupped her jaw. "What happened, darling?"

Flames smoldered in his eyes, but his touch and voice were gentle. His rage wasn't at her. *It wasn't at her.* Relief dissolved the starch in her knees, and she would have fallen had he not caught her around the waist, steadying her against his solid strength.

"The punch," she managed. "I think... it was drugged. The next thing I knew, I woke up here."

Hell-fire leapt in his eyes. "Can you stand on your own?" he bit out.

She nodded.

He spun to face the footman, who, obviously sensing the direction the wind was blowing, had scrambled to his feet. He held his hands out in front of him as he backed away.

"Now look here, my lord. It wasn't my fault. Your wife wanted it—"

Marcus' fist flew out, connecting with a loud crack.

"My nose! You've broken my bleeding nose—" The footman groaned, doubling over from the punch to his ribs.

"I'm going to kill you, you bastard," Marcus snarled.

The footman tried to fight back. His attempts were as ineffectual as a cat batting its paws at a lion—and an enraged king of the jungle at that. Stumbling back from another of Marcus' powerful blows, he gasped, "It wasn't my fault. It was Lady Ashley's. Promised me a hundred quid, she did, to drug the punch. To set this all up."

Anger swept through Penny, clearing away some of her wooziness. She'd guessed as much, but hearing confirmation of Cora's vile plot made her hands curl at her sides. Cora's cheeks were as pallid as her dress, her eyes darting, and, without a word, she dashed out of the gallery.

Marcus had the servant by the neck, pinning him to the wall. "What drug was used?"

"Just a sleeping draught," the bastard gasped. "The mistress uses it herself, said it wouldn't harm the lady. Just put double the dose, she said, and bring her up to the gallery and make it look like a tryst. Nothing happened, I swear. I was just following orders—"

Marcus' fist plowed into the footman's jaw, and, with a feeble moan, the latter slid down the wall, crumpled and unconscious.

Marcus strode over to Penny. The battle light hadn't left his eyes, and she knew the effort it cost him to gentle his voice as he said, "Let's get you dressed and out of here."

She nodded, and he helped her into her gown, straightening her coiffure.

"Ready?" he said.

"Yes. Marcus?"

"Yes, love?"

"Thank you," she whispered.

He touched her cheek, self-recrimination darkening his eyes. "Don't thank me. It's my fault. I should have protected you—I just never guessed that Cora Ashley would be capable of such deviousness."

Cora's maliciousness didn't surprise Penny at all... but she decided to let it go.

For now.

"Thank you for rescuing me anyway," she said softly. "Most of all, thank you for trusting me."

Some of the brooding left his gaze. Keeping one arm around her shoulders, he touched the ruby necklace at her throat.

"Don't you know that your worth is beyond compare, Penny? I trust and love you with everything that I am," he said.

She didn't know how she'd come to deserve such a husband. But he was hers. All hers.

"I love you so much, Marcus." Her eyes welled, her balance wavering.

He swept her up into his arms. Kissed her tenderly. "Let's go home."

EPILOGUE

Several days later, on Christmas Day, the Blackwoods' drawing room was the site of cozy pandemonium. Against Marcus' wishes—he'd been adamant that Penny should stay in bed and rest after her ordeal—Penny had arranged a little party. She'd wanted to celebrate the holiday with their closest friends and family.

Now she was sitting with Emma and Thea at a window seat, watching as plump snowflakes drifted lazily outside. Inside, the fire leapt merrily, conversation and children's laughter flowing through the halls, the scent of gingerbread and spiced Yuletide posset warming the air.

"Thank goodness you've recovered," Thea said.

"I feel absolutely fine." Penny gave a wry smile. "In fact, I slept like a babe the day after the Ashleys' ball, and now I'm more rested than I've been in ages."

"I cannot believe the sheer maliciousness of Cora Ashley." Emma's chestnut curls bobbed as she shook her head. "Imagine hatching such a devious plot."

"At least her punishment fits the crime," Thea said philosophically.

The day after the party, an incensed Marcus had gone to speak

with Lord Ashley. He'd informed the earl of his countess' trans-
gressions, and, according to Marcus' report, Ashley's reaction had
been neither shocked nor even particularly caring.

I'll take care of it, the earl had said in a bored voice.

Three days after that, Cora Ashley had been shipped off to a
distant property in Ireland. According to the *on dit*, there was no
return date. Privately, Marcus told Penny that he thought it was
good riddance, and Cora deserved her banishment.

Penny, for her part, wasn't quite as magnanimous as Marcus.
The bloody wench had drugged her, set her up, and *tried to steal
her husband*: to her mind, that merited a fair bit more than some
jaunt in the Irish countryside. Which was why she'd had a little
gift planted in the lady's carriage. Just a dozen or so of Cora's
favorite eight-legged friends to keep her company on the road.

Feeling generous, however, Penny hadn't included any poisonous varieties.

See? She had turned over a new leaf.

"I'm just thankful that no scandal has resulted from all of
this," she said. "I shudder to think what might have happened if
anyone else had come upon that dreadful scene."

Even though she had the precious gift of Marcus' trust, the
last thing she wanted was to drag the Blackwood name through
the mud. Especially since she and her mama-in-law were on pecu-
liarly good terms these days. Upon arrival today, the old dragon
had inspected her up and down and then patted her on the cheek,
saying gruffly, "Always knew you were a hardy bloom, my dear. Just
like me. Now fetch me some of that Yuletide posset—and mind
you don't skimp on the Madeira."

"As for the lack of scandal, you might have Violet to thank,"
Emma muttered.

"Violet?" Penny said in surprise. "What does she have to do
with this?"

Emma and Thea exchanged glances.

"I must have your most solemn promise that you won't tell anyone else—except your husband, of course," Emma said.

Growing more intrigued by the moment, Penny nodded.

Thea leaned forward, her voice hushed. "You do know what happened to Viscount Carlisle at the Ashleys' Ball?"

She did. The whole *ton* did.

Somehow, the proud and dignified Scotsman had managed to land on his arse... *in* the champagne fountain. How the mighty had fallen.

"I heard he created quite a splash." Penny couldn't help herself.

Emma gave her a wry look. "You and every tattle rag in London have used that line. At any rate, his mishap proved advantageous in one respect: it drew the attention away from Cora Ashley's machinations upstairs. Everyone was focused on Carlisle's accident and took no notice of your departure."

"The only problem is," Thea said in a whisper, "we don't think it was an accident."

"It wasn't?" Penny said, puzzled.

"Violet had something to do with it," Emma said.

"Never say she *pushed* Carlisle into the fountain?" A startled laugh escaped Penny.

Gnawing on her lower lip, Emma said, "Vi wouldn't give us the exact details, but she was quite distressed over the whole business."

"And it takes *a lot* to distress Violet," Thea said, her hazel eyes brimming with concern.

"Oh, dear." Sobering, Penny hoped that disaster didn't lay in wait. She couldn't imagine a more unlikely and volatile pairing than between the reckless hoyden and the haughty Scot. "You don't think there's anything... well, *going on* between your sister and Carlisle? I thought she was enamored of his younger brother Wickham?"

"You never know with Violet," the duchess said with a sigh. "Which is precisely why we're worried."

———

Later on that evening, Marcus cuddled Penny against his side. They were in bed, naked, their skin still warm and damp from the exertions of their recent lovemaking. Although, in truth, his wife had done most of the work. He traced the sweet shape of her lips and decided he wanted the same thing for Christmas every year.

As if reading his thoughts, Penny murmured against his chest, "Merry Christmas, Lord Blackwood."

"Merry Christmas, Lady Blackwood." He played with a long raven tress.

"What did you think of the party? Did you enjoy it?"

Smiling, he said, "It was splendid. You did a marvelous job, love. Although next year I vote we do away with the Twelfth cake."

To entertain the children, his wife had decided to buck tradition and serve a Twelfth cake on Christmas Day. Embedded in the beautifully iced confection had been a small golden crown: the guest who found the crown in his or her slice got to be king or queen for the day, with the accompanying right to order around the other guests.

Owen had crowed with delight when he'd been crowned king.

His brothers had been less pleased.

"I'm afraid we raised a tyrant. Or, more accurately, three of them." Penny traced delicate circles on his chest with her index finger. "I do hope they'll be on better behavior when Agatha meets them next month."

Knowing how much his wife was looking forward to Agatha's visit, Marcus grinned. "You just don't want to admit that I was right and you were wrong when it comes to the boys being little hellions. Might as well admit defeat now, love: Agatha's going to side with me, and you know it."

"All right, I admit it. You win." Penny raised her head, smiling ruefully. Her new ruby and diamond earbobs, the Christmas gift he'd given her to match her necklace, caught the light of the fire and glittered richly against her dark hair.

He touched one earring. "These suit you."

"I love them, and I love you. Which reminds me—I've a gift for you, too." She left the bed to retrieve it.

Watching the delightful sway of his wife's ass, he waggled his brows and said, "Didn't you just give it to me?"

She tossed him a saucy wink over her shoulder. "That was your Christmas present." She plucked something from her vanity and returned to the bed, handing him a black velvet box. "This is to celebrate our anniversary."

It struck him then.

"The first time we met was on Christmas," he murmured. "All those years ago."

She smiled. "Precisely. Now aren't you going to open the box?"

He sat up and removed the lid. A handsome gold watch lay nestled against the white satin lining. Lifting it out, he admired it, saying, "Thank you, darling. It's a fine piece."

"It's engraved," she said.

He turned it over, and his throat clogged. He ran his thumb over the elegant script.

Together through every season.

Setting the watch carefully back into the box, he pulled Penny into his arms and poured his love for her into a long, sweet kiss. They were both breathless when it ended.

"You like it then?" Penny said, her cheeks flushed.

"I adore it. And I adore you." He tucked a silken curl behind her ear. "But I'm afraid I didn't get an anniversary present for you. We shall rectify that oversight first thing tomorrow. You can have anything you want."

"*Anything* I want?" Her eyes sparkled more brilliantly than the rubies.

"Anything within my power to give," he said solemnly.

She leaned in, bringing her lips to his ear. There, she whispered her heart's desire.

He gave a husky laugh. Staring into his beloved's eyes, he murmured, "As to that, I can make no guarantees, my darling, other than to do my very best."

He kissed her and, as he'd promised, did his very best.

Twice.

And because Marcus was a gentleman of honor, one who kept his word to his cherished wife, nine months later Miss Georgiana Flora Aileen Harrington was welcomed joyfully into the world.

ACKNOWLEDGMENTS

I'm blessed to have so many amazing people in my corner. Tina, Diane, Carrie, The Montauk Eight, Jesse: each of you support me and my writing in your own unique way, and I'm so grateful to have you in my life!

To my family, who is there with me every step of the way.

To my readers, who make it possible for me to do what I love.

And to Brian, to whom this book is dedicated: for all the seasons we've been through together and all the ones to come. I'm so lucky, babe.

ABOUT THE AUTHOR

USA Today & International Bestselling Author Grace Callaway writes hot and heart-melting historical romance filled with mystery and adventure. Her debut novel was a Romance Writers of America® Golden Heart® Finalist and a #1 National Regency Bestseller, and her subsequent novels have topped national and international bestselling lists. She is the winner of the Daphne du Maurier Award for Excellence in Mystery and Suspense, the Maggie Award for Excellence in Historical Romance, the Golden Leaf, and the Passionate Plume Award. She holds a doctorate in clinical psychology from the University of Michigan and lives with her family in a valley close to the sea. When she's not writing, she enjoys dancing, exploring the great outdoors with her rescue pup, and going on adapted adventures with her special son.

Stay connected with Grace!

Newsletter: gracecallaway.com/newsletter

Reader Group:
    facebook.com/groups/gracecallawaybookclub/

f facebook.com/GraceCallawayBooks
BB bookbub.com/authors/grace-callaway
O instagram.com/gracecallawaybooks
a amazon.com/author/gracecallaway